THE NIGHT RIDERS

Jim Gatlin rode into Cedar Creek hunting the man who had framed him for a crime he didn't commit. Meanwhile, Pinkerton agent Charlie Pine had located the real train robber, a man named Hood. Outlaws Hidalgo, Wilson and River were also after Hood, for the fortune locked up in his home. But why was Marshal Silva making a secret of Hood's whereabouts? Against overwhelming odds, Gatlin would face a bloody showdown, needing all his skill and courage to unlock a shocking secret.

MATT LAIDLAW

◆

THE NIGHT RIDERS

Complete and Unabridged

LINFORD
Leicester

First published in Great Britain in 2006 by
Robert Hale Limited
London

First Linford Edition
published 2007
by arrangement with
Robert Hale Limited
London

British Library CIP Data

Laidlaw, Matt
    The night riders.—Large print ed.—
Linford western library
1. Western stories
2. Large type books
I. Title
813.5'4 [F]

ISBN 978–1–84782–015–0

Published by
F. A. Thorpe (Publishing)
Anstey, Leicestershire

Set by Words & Graphics Ltd.
Anstey, Leicestershire
Printed and bound in Great Britain by
T. J. International Ltd., Padstow, Cornwall

This book is printed on acid-free paper

For the Ryder boys
Peter, the lawman
(Royal Military Police),
Graham Lee on the chuck wagon
(head chef)
Both fine grandsons.

PROLOGUE

The cantina was a sod-roof adobe hovel with one opening and no windows and had been old when Mexican president Santa Anna was waging a losing war against the United States. A rusting cannon ball was lodged in the outside wall. Blackened bullet holes were pock marks on the interior walls between torn, yellowing posters and reward notices and the huge cracked mirror behind the bar. That bar had been fashioned out of timber scavenged from ships wrecked on the Gulf coast, the tables from ships' barrels. Smoke from a cracked, pot-bellied iron stove mingled with the fumes from cigars, cigarettes and cigarillos to create an atmosphere a man could chew and spit out into the chopped off tin cans serving as leaky cuspidors. The atmosphere was kept ripe by a sheet of stained canvas that was used for a door. It hung limp and heavy in the hot air, weighed down by filth.

The night before the three outlaws rode into the south-Texas trading post, the fat Mexican owner had used both barrels of a sawn-off shotgun to cut a Texan troublemaker down to size. The double charge of buckshot had ripped open the renegade's belly and the dying man's bright blood had splashed the bar and the barrels that served as tables and added flavour and colour to the glasses of cheap tequila and mescal. It had also dried in blackened runs on the mirror's fly-blown glass, and liberally spattered the owner's greasy countenance in which black eyes gleamed like wet river stones. That unshaven face remained unwashed.

'Maybe,' River said ruminatively, 'he's goin' by what he sees in that mirror. A man looks in that, he'd figure the stains're on the glass, not his face.'

Hidalgo grinned. 'If that's so, why

has he not washed the mirror?'

'Why don't both of you quit idle speculation about a fat, no-account greaser's personal hygiene, and get down to talking business.'

The man who had spoken last was a lanky, fair-haired gunslinger by the name of Wilson. It was a simple name, but he'd long ago figured that if he plugged enough men then one day he'd be as notorious as William Bonney but without the childish sobriquet.

So far, he'd sent five or six dead men to boot hill — he couldn't be exactly sure of the numbers. That was satisfying, but notoriety and the cash he'd hoped would come with the killings were both eluding him: he had lately begun to realize that shooting penniless drifters full of holes merely to boost the name of Wilson was a losing game.

'Business,' Hidalgo said. 'What damn business? So far, you've told us nothing.'

'What I've told you is I was passed information by a man who got locked up in the pen a week before I walked free.'

'And now you've been free a week of your own — and still we're waiting.'

'So now the waiting's over. I tell you what I know. You get excited thinking of the rich pickings. This time tomorrow, we head north.'

'North?' River said. 'Where north?'

'Wyoming,' Wilson said. 'There's a man living easy up there. Ten years ago, he was the brains behind a big train robbery. That train was taking cash to banks all along the Atchison Topeka line. But what that man did was so big, yet so easy, it taught him a lesson. Banks, he figured, were easy pickings. There and then, he vowed no bank would ever get a sniff of the money he stole. He's got a big house. He keeps a safe in his bedroom. You want more cash than you've seen in your whole damn life — that's where it is.'

'Yesterday I was robbing banks,' Hidalgo said. 'Tomorrow I ride to Wyoming to rob bedrooms.'

'Just the one,' Wilson said. 'Then we retire, say goodbye to stinking bars run by bloodstained Mexicans, dead worms floating in bad liquor, air so bad a man could choke to death.'

And he spat wetly, deliberately missing the nearest cuspidor.

PART ONE

1

Jim Gatlin rode down into Cedar Creek close to midnight, his slicker shiny in the light from the town's swinging oil lamps. Warm rain was being driven by a strong north-westerly wind moaning down from the wooded hills, setting false fronts and signs rattling and creaking like a bad carnival band all the way down the steep twisting slope of Main Street. His roan picked its way delicately through deep ruts slick with mud. Light glowed in the open doorway of the general store, and he guessed the owner was up late checking his stock. The hitch rail in front of the saloon was unoccupied, the saloon itself in darkness except for a light at the rear seen through one of the dusty windows.

As he rode past, a dark shape appeared in that window, and stayed there. Watching, Gatlin thought, and he

9

cursed softly. Without haste, he turned his head and looked the other way.

The time of his arrival had been chosen with care. This late, he knew most people would be at home in bed, business premises locked and deserted, Main Street empty. That had been a certainty, the heavy early-summer rain a stroke of luck. Put the two together and he knew few people were likely to witness his arrival; if he was seen, he knew damn well he would not be recognized. The poor likeness on wanted dodgers — if any were still around — would be more than nine years old. His soaking wet Stetson was pulled well down, and three-days' dark stubble altered his looks and disguised the lower half of his face as effectively as a bandit's neckerchief.

He was reasonably familiar with the town's layout from talks with Charlie Pine. Pine had told him exactly where the marshal's office was located. It happened to be at the bottom of the hill and directly opposite the hotel, Charlie said, where Gatlin should take a room while he took stock and got his bearings. Gatlin looked on that situation as both good and bad. Risky, because if anyone was going to recognize him it would be the marshal with those old reward notices gathering dust on his desk and their details lodged in his memory. But handy, too, because from a first-floor window he would be able to keep track of the marshal's comings and goings.

Gatlin hugged the side of the street, ducking his head so that his dripping hat brim kept the worst of the rain out of his eyes. He'd left the general store and the saloon fifty yards behind him. Here, by the stone building that was the Cedar Creek bank, the street went off to the right at a shallow angle and plunged steeply downhill before levelling out in the trees on the town's outskirts. As Gatlin eased the roan around the bend he could see, at the bottom of the hill, a single hitched horse dozing in the yellow light spilling from another stone building on the left, the vapour from its warm body like dispersing gunsmoke. The jail, and marshal's office. Either the marshal or one of his deputies on duty. Opposite the jail, a three-storey timber structure clinging to the wooded hillside seemed to sag in upon itself in the pouring rain. Even from a distance Gatlin could see the sign clinging to its front, the writing on it weather-worn.

Cedar Creek Hotel.

Beyond it, on the same block, the town's livery stable. A café. Between those two another business premises, with bold lettering high on the false front: Josh Notion. Guns. Pistols. Ammunition.

Gatlin took a deep breath, brought a hand out from under the slicker and dashed the water from his eyes.

There was no sign of movement at the jail as he drew near, but this was the first test of the many that were sure to come. This was when an empty street worked against him, when a solitary rider would not go unnoticed; when a keen-eyed town marshal would register the arrival of a trail-weary stranger and make a mental note to pay that man a visit.

Gatlin thought absently of the dark shape standing without movement in the saloon's window. Then he heeled the roan forward and rode at an angle across the rutted street, away from the jail and towards the livery barn.

Halfway there he looked back at the jail. Through rain drifting across the open doorway he could make out an oil lamp suspended over a desk heaped high with papers, a newfangled typewriter, shiny boots crossed at the ankles, long legs and body leading to a blurred face and a thread of smoke rising from an unseen cigarette or pipe to curl around the lamp.

Then he was all the way across the street and a little way downhill and the angle of view had changed. He dismissed the marshal from his mind. The livery barn's big doors were open.

He rode straight in to the smell of fresh clean straw, dragged the hostler out of his warm office and arranged for the care of his horse. Money exchanged hands. That done, Gatlin unstrapped his bedroll and slung it over his shoulder as he walked back up the street to the hotel.

The plank walk was wet, the boards warped. When he grasped the knob and pushed open the door he got the feeling knob and door were about to come off in his hand. He shut it behind him, heard it rattle and the latch click and stood for a moment as his eyes adjusted to the dim light.

It was a small entrance hallway, with a passage leading to the rear of the building, stairs ascending to the upper floors. A half open roll-top desk stood against one wall, the roll-top's slats coming off the canvas. On the writing surface Gatlin saw an open book — the register, he guessed — and a flat-domed brass bell, the kind you hit with the flat of your hand.

He trailed water across threadbare carpet to the desk and hit the bell. It clanked mournfully. But his arrival had been heard. The opening and closing of the door had been enough to alert the hotel's owner, and footsteps were slopping down the passage.

He was a gaunt and bent old man, half dressed, with a straggling moustache and glittering eyes that peered at Gatlin from the black sockets of a skull decorated with strands of thin hair. An old percussion six-gun was poked into the waistband of baggy black trousers. The front of his torn undershirt was stained with tobacco juice.

'Rooms're a dollar a day,' the apparition said, in a voice like hoarse breathing. 'In advance.'

'For a front room, first floor, and some secrecy,' Gatlin said. 'I'll give you five dollars now. If I'm here longer, I'll pay for each extra day. You keep your mouth shut, I'll double what I've paid when I leave.'

'You're safe enough. My eyes are

bad, my memory ain't what it was and too many questions leave me confused. Sign the book, or let me get back to sleep.'

Gatlin reached under the slicker to his money belt and jingled five coins on the desk. There was a scratchy pen, and a bottle of ink. He scrawled his name, Jim Gatlin, making the signature almost unreadable. He hid a wry smile as the proprietor swung the book to scrutinize the page. The old man tossed him a world-weary glance, then poked dirty fingers into a pigeon hole and handed Gatlin a key with a tag.

The stairs were dark and creaking, the hand rail greasy. At the top there was a right turn into a narrow corridor stinking of mildew and coal oil. A lamp smoked on a table at the far end. Gatlin looked at the key's wooden tag. Number two. He opened the second door along. Went in. Closed the door. Flipped his hat onto the chair, shrugged out of the wet slicker and draped it over the chair's back, dropped his bedroll on the cot and hitched his Colt .45 to a comfortable position on his right thigh.

The light from the jail shone through rain-beaded glass and picked out the network of cracks in a ceiling stained a dull tobacco colour by years of cigarette smoke. Gatlin brushed past the cot and stood to one side of the window. When he hooked back the filthy net curtain and looked down he could see the sloping, rutted street shining in the rain, the far plank walk, the front of the jail and its iron roof. The door was still open but he was too high to see in as far as the desk; couldn't tell if the man was still sprawled there, enjoying his cigarette.

Then his eyes were caught by movement directly below him. Breath hissed through his nostrils as he watched the bent figure cloaked in a blanket step down off the plank walk, start across the road, then pause to look back at Gatlin's window.

The old man. After that quick backward look he turned away and seemed to dance across the ruts and the mud like a sprightly gnome, finally disappearing through the open door of the jail.

Thoughtfully, Gatlin let the curtain fall. When he turned, the jail's light was strong enough to throw his faint shadow across the ceiling's cracks. With sudden insight he saw them as rivers and trails criss-crossing a stained parchment map of the West, his shadow the giant shape of a man covering the route of an epic ride.

That long ride from Santa Fe had been the first leg of a journey to reclaim his soul. Over several weeks the roan had borne him through Pueblo and Colorado Springs, through Cheyenne and Laramie, along the eastern slopes of the Rattlesnake Range and across the Middle and North Forks of the Powder River. Cedar Creek was a settlement in the foothills of the Big Horn Mountains close to Crazy Woman Creek. He had camped in those hills for a full day and ridden to town when the time was right.

The long first leg had been tough, but not beyond the capabilities of the average, hard-bitten range rider. What the second leg entailed was so far beyond Gatlin's imagination that he had spent little time in contemplation.

Now? Well, now he knew for sure that he was in Cedar Creek — but that was all he knew. Until tomorrow.

Well, maybe not all. What he now knew for sure was that if his scrawled signature had been deciphered by the old man's weak eyes, and if his memory lasted until he got across the street, the marshal sitting in his cosy office was listening to the news of a certain Jim Gatlin's arrival in Cedar Creek. Which suggested that what happened next could prove very interesting.

Pensively, thinking of the task he had set himself and what lay behind it, Gatlin sat down on the bed and pulled off his wet boots. The rain had soaked through to his thick socks. He peeled them off, padded across the room and draped them over the edge of the

19

stained basin on the wash stand.

He was standing like that, looking at his reflection in the cracked mirror, when outside in the corridor a board creaked. With a low, tight exclamation of chagrin, Gatlin drew his six-gun and swung to face the door.

2

Josh Notion was sitting at the rough timber bar staring broodingly into his glass of warm beer. Light from the street struggled in through the saloon's filthy windows to touch his broad back, the butt of a six-gun, the twists of the plaited leather band encircling his stained felt hat. The yellow light shining through the open door leading to the back room picked out high cheekbones, the black patch over his left eye, the gleam of white teeth under a bushy moustache.

'We've seen strangers ride into town before today,' Notion said, without looking up. 'I've never mentioned it to Hood — never had cause to, never considered it my obligation.'

'Yeah — but tonight I've got me a feeling.'

The woman who had spoken was on

a high stool against the shelves behind the bar, in deep shadow. There was a sense of voluptuousness and, without looking directly, Notion could see the faint sheen of brassy hair, the glint of eyes like cool sapphires, the occasional glitter of gold rings and glass as she sipped whiskey.

Ten minutes ago, Notion had gone to the window to watch the stranger in the shiny slicker ride down the street in the slashing rain, and had immediately dismissed him as another drifter, an itinerant looking for a dry bed before pushing on north to Montana, or south to New Mexico. That was his opinion, even after he'd taken time to consider — but if Kitty Mac had got one of her feelings . . .

'Don't ask me why but, according to Belinda, more than a year ago now Hood started actin' worried, eyes distant, jumpin' at the slightest sound,' Notion mused. 'I suppose for his daughter's sake I should take a ride in the rain, tell him what I've seen. But it's

22

past midnight already, and that'd mean waking him up.'

'You know what I think of the man,' Kitty said. 'Belinda's a fine young woman, but if her pa got boiled in oil I'd be the first to raise a glass at his passing. Asking me to help him would be a waste of breath. But I can't say what's right or wrong. If you think dragging him out of bed is looking out for that daughter of his . . . '

'I'd still like it if we had more to go on.' Notion took a pull at his beer, thinking. 'What about Haydn Crawford?'

Kitty's grunt was disparaging. 'He may head the town council, but he's still just another puppet.'

'All right — then are you still hanging on to that dodger you got from Silva?'

Kitty Mac slid off the stool with a rustle and a waft of heady perfume. When she planted her glass on the bar she stepped into the weak light from windows and back room and Notion

23

was dazzled by the full splendour of her flouncy yellow dress with frills and pearl buttons, her painted lips, the thick blonde hair held high with tortoiseshell Spanish combs. He caught himself wondering where she strapped her favoured ivory-handled derringer, and in his imagination pictured a wide lace garter circling a thigh like a pale tree trunk . . .

Paper rustled as Kitty rummaged under the bar and slapped a torn and rumpled wanted dodger in front of Notion. He spun it the right way up and looked at the crude representation of a thin face darkened by a couple of days of stubble. He shook his head.

'From all that picture tells us, it could be me or you,' he said, and now a slow grin split his lean face as he looked directly at the voluptuous owner of the Wayfarer saloon. 'Maybe I should get Jax Silva himself to sort this out.'

'How?'

'Best way,' Notion said, 'is for the marshal to walk across the street and confront the man.'

'What, ask him straight out if he's Jim Gatlin come a-hunting?'

'A man hiding behind a badge can do that and maybe get away with it.'

'Hiding? For Silva, that wouldn't take much of a badge.' Kitty's eyes twinkled. 'Maybe you should go with him, hold his hand.'

'If he talks to the man we believe is Gatlin, I'll tag along.'

'And if Silva finds my feelings are right, you'll have some justification for hauling Hood out of bed.'

Notion waited as Kitty Mac nursed her drink and thought for a moment, mentally putting her intuition to the test. He was proud that this feisty woman considered him to be a close friend, and admired his ability to distance himself from Hood. But he knew she was well aware that, if things were not to his liking, Hood could make it uncomfortable for them and the rest of the inhabitants of Cedar Creek.

And still she didn't speak.

Restlessly, he walked across to the window. The lashing rain had cooled the window. Notion scrubbed away the condensation with his sleeve and looked down the hill. As he watched, a bent figure with a blanket over its head emerged from the hotel and scuttled off the plank walk into the muddy street. Halfway across, it stopped, turned, and looked back at an upstairs window before hurrying the rest of the way. Notion thought he saw a pale face split by the smudge of a moustache.

When he returned to the bar, Kitty met his gaze and her eyes softened. Then she tossed back the last of her whiskey, pursed ruby-red lips and nodded.

'Play safe, Josh. Go tell him.'

'Things have changed. That's already been done.'

3

Jim Gatlin stood barefoot on cold boards, the street lighting at his back. Carefully, he eased back the hammer of his Colt. Mentally distancing himself from the moan of the wind, the rattle of rain on window and roof, he strained his ears for a repeat of the sound that had alerted him.

Again it came: a board creaking in the passageway. And this time it was followed by a distinct footfall, and another, each one drawing closer to room number two. Then, as Gatlin's nerves sang like taut piano wire, the tension was abruptly snapped by a loud rapping on the door.

Gatlin felt the pistol jerk in his hand. There was a faint tremor in the muscles along his jaw. He clenched his teeth.

'Yeah,' he said tightly; and he lifted the six-gun and levelled it at the door's thin timber. 'It's not locked, come on in.'

There was no reply. In the silence Gatlin heard a faint metallic squeal and saw the door knob begin to turn. It turned all the way, stopped. There was a breathless pause. Then there was the sound of something solid hitting the heavy door. It exploded open, crashed against the wall. In the opening a small man stood with one hand on his shoulder. The other held a gun like a medium-sized cannon.

'Jesus Christ, Charlie,' Gatlin said, 'are you trying to get yourself killed?'

★   ★   ★

The oil lamp was lit, the threadbare curtains closed. On the washstand a half-full bottle of whiskey stood alongside two glasses. Jim Gatlin was stretched out on the cot, long legs crossed, fingers laced behind his head. He thought, with some amusement, that Charlie Pine was the only man he knew who carried jolt glasses in his saddle-bag. But Charlie Pine was a most unusual man.

Pine was seated on the rickety chair looking with interest at a cotton sack Gatlin had, moments before, taken out of his bed roll.

Stencilled across the sack were the words ATCHISON TOPEKA.

'Must have been one of the first bags that railroad had made,' Charlie said. 'The men who stole the cash it was carrying were just about this country's first train robbers.'

'But not just the one bag.'

'No, it was more like fifty of those sacks.'

'And not taken by you.'

Gatlin took a deep breath. 'If it was me, you wouldn't be here.'

'No.' Pine shook his head. 'And now I am here — is there anything I can say that'll change your mind?'

Gatlin frowned. 'Why would you want to do that?'

'Because what you have in mind is

cold-blooded murder.'

Gatlin hesitated. 'No. I told you right at the beginning, a full year ago, retribution is what I have in mind. A reckoning, an eye for an eye — and then only if I'm one hundred per cent certain and even then I've still to decide what to do. A man planted some of those sacks in my home and tipped off the county sheriff. I lost eight years of my life. While I was rotting inside the Texas State Pen my wife died in childbirth, my widowed ma died of a broken heart and the house my pa had built with his bare hands was burned to the ground.'

'Maybe,' Charlie Pine said, 'I should have kept my mouth shut.'

'Would've done no good.' Gatlin's shake of the head was emphatic. 'You've brought matters to a head by finding the man — '

'Sixty per cent sure,' Pine said, 'which leaves one hell of a margin for error.'

'Yeah, well, one way or another I'll

get there in the end. If you're sixty per cent sure, you've saved forty per cent of my time.'

'But maybe shortened a man's life.'

'A wicked man's life,' Gatlin corrected. 'And it's not done yet. He won't lie down without a fight. And I'd guess he's recruited some hard men for his personal protection.'

'What I think,' Charlie Pine said, 'is you have too high an opinion of yourself.'

'That was never true. And what pride I did have was painfully removed by prison guards,' Gatlin said.

Pine tossed the sack onto the bed and went to the washstand. Whiskey gurgled into the glasses. He handed one to Gatlin. For several minutes they were silent, Gatlin settled and ready for sleep now that he had good company, Charlie Pine restless, clearly bothered by what Gatlin assumed to be confused feelings of loyalty and guilt.

Both of them heard the hard slamming of a door.

They exchanged glances.

Gatlin came off the cot with one smooth swing of the legs. Pine crossed swiftly to the window and lifted the curtain.

'Three men crossing the street from the jail. The tall one's dressed like he's been down to the store and bought new clothes. He's also wearing a badge.'

4

'What do you mean, explain my reasons for being here?' Jim Gatlin said.

'Well, I don't have the kind of suspicions about you a man can nail down,' Marshal Jax Silva said, 'but if keeping the peace means running disreputable strangers out of town . . . '

He left the words unfinished, his meaning clear.

Backed up by a whipcord thin man with seething eyes and supple leather gloves pulled tight on restless hands, another unshaven character with a shotgun carried slack in his hand and a look of mild amusement, the marshal of Cedar Creek had knocked once on Gatlin's door and walked in. Tall and ramrod-straight and of an age somewhere between forty and sixty, he had a beard razor-trimmed round the outline of his square jaw, shrewd grey eyes and pomaded black hair curling over the collar of a shirt with a hand-stitched front worn under a fancy cowhide vest. His Stetson was white, darkened by the rain. The six-gun in its oiled leather holster had an engraved ivory butt.

A man, Gatlin thought, who is handsomely paid to do a job that has little to do with keeping the peace but a lot to do with protecting the interests of a man with money and influence.

'If being disreputable was a crime, most of the men I've met would be in jail,' Gatlin said. 'But that's not the issue here. You asked me my reasons for being in Cedar Creek. Well, why I'm here is none of your business, and if that touches a raw nerve in a man who's maybe too big for his boots — '

'Forget my feelings, son. And dish out the insults whenever you feel inclined, because I've heard them all and they change nothing. I do my job, and that means abiding by rules laid down by the men who pay my wages.'

'The town council?'

'In a nutshell.'

'Every man-jack of them dancing to the tune of the head man, the town mayor.'

Jax Silva chuckled, but the cynical eyes hardened.

'Ain't that always the case?'

'You asked why I'm here. What would you say if I told you I had unfinished business with this . . . powerful man?'

'Yeah, well, you see that's where we hit problems.' Silva changed tack, shifted his gaze to Charlie Pine. 'I know you, don't I? You're that Pinkerton op working out of Denver, been doing some snoopin' around, asking a whole heap of questions. All this time I've been wondering why. I guess I've got my answer.'

'Nothing's changed,' Gatlin said, echoing the marshal's words.

'It's about to,' Silva said.

A signal was passed that Gatlin missed. Suddenly the man holding the shotgun had cocked the murderous weapon and rammed the twin muzzles hard up against Charlie Pine's head. Pine winced, tried to pull away, and was stopped by the gunman's warning glare. Distracted, caught cold, Gatlin moved too late. Marshal Jax Silva's fancy six-gun seemed to leap from holster to hand. In that instant Gatlin found himself looking down the barrel of a cocked revolver.

The wiry man stepped forward. A strange light was burning in his eyes. He reached out a hand, plucked Gatlin's six-gun from his holster and tossed it to Silva. The marshal caught it with his free hand and grinned.

'Makes it easy. I never did understand why a man burns his initials into the butt of his gun.' He nodded to the man with the shotgun. 'You keep that Greener on the Pinkerton boy, Mundt. This is Green's play, not mine, so let him set things up.'

Stepping lightly, Green crossed the board floor.

'Stand up.'

Charlie Pine looked at Gatlin. His expression was unreadable. He sighed, and came up off the hard chair.

Green stepped forward and took hold of Pine's right wrist with both his gloved hands. Instinctively, Pine clenched his fist. The other man, Mundt, turned Pine roughly. Green tightened his grip, dragged the Pinkerton man over to the wash stand and brought his hand down to rest on the solid timber surface. Mundt had followed. With a grin, he lifted the shotgun vertically and brought the butt slamming down on Pine's closed fist.

Gatlin's skin prickled. He heard bones snap. Pine grunted, and breath hissed through his clenched teeth. When Green released his wrist and stepped away the Pinkerton man turned and sagged back against the wash stand. His face was white. He'd bitten into his lower lip. Blood trickled down his chin.

Lightly, easily, Green swung a short fast right hook that caught Pine under the right eye. His head cracked against the wall. The water jug toppled over in the basin. Green spat on his gloved hand and moved away from the stricken operative.

Gatlin stared narrow-eyed at Silva. 'What the hell are you doing?'

'Work it out,' Silva said. 'A man don't do that much damage to his fist by accident. What happens is, he gets in a fight. The bones get broken when he throws a punch.'

This time, Gatlin saw Silva's signal. It was an almost imperceptible nod.

Then Green was all over him.

With the back of his legs up against the cot and under threat from Silva's six-gun and Mundt's cocked shotgun, Gatlin could do nothing but defend. Green directed a fierce barrage of punches at his face. When Gatlin tried to smother his arms, he danced back. Then he was in again. Left, right, hook, jab. One jolting right hand split Gatlin's lip and he felt the trickle of hot blood, the taste of copper in his mouth. A vicious blow loosened a tooth. Another punch crushed his nose. His eyes streamed tears. An uppercut exploded under his chin and his teeth snapped shut. Then a powerful right came out of nowhere, cracked against his right eye and he went sprawling backwards across the cot.

Head singing, he heard Silva snap a command. A hand reached out, grabbed a handful of his hair and dragged him to a sitting position. His head was released. He leaned forward, elbows on knees, and spat blood on the floor. When he looked up, blearily, Silva was waiting.

'This is how it goes,' the marshal said, and he pouched his own six-gun and dangled Gatlin's initialled pistol by the trigger guard. 'You and the Pinkerton man disagreed, got into a fight. One look at your faces, and it's clear who was coming out on top. Only then Pine broke his fist on your hard skull, and that let you in. You pulled your pistol, and you shot him dead.'

Silva socked the butt of Gatlin's pistol into his palm with a deft spin, drew back the hammer and levelled the six-gun at the Pinkerton man.

'No,' Gatlin said. 'You can't do that.'

'What's stopping me? You?' Silva shook his head. 'I don't think so.'

'All right.' Gatlin sucked breath in through his mashed lips. 'What do you want, Marshal? Whatever it is you want, I'll do it. Just — put down that pistol.'

'You leave town, now — or Pine dies.'

Then the lean man called Green spoke up.

'We've gone to a lot of trouble to set the stage, Silva. Why back off now? Plug the Pinkerton man, hang the other feller at dawn and your troubles are over. You let him go, he'll come back poking his nose in as sure as a hog roots in mud.'

Gatlin dragged the back of his hand across his bloody chin.

'You're wrong. Why would I come back — ?'

'You've got unfinished business,'

40

Silva said, 'with a man not yet named.'

And then Silva did something that was completely unexpected. He stepped forward to reach across Gatlin, and from the cot he picked up the bag with ATCHISON TOPEKA stencilled across it in bold black letters. Still keeping Gatlin's pistol levelled at Pine, he passed the bag slowly in front of Gatlin's bloody face.

Gatlin forced a bitter smile. 'I guess that business will have to stay unfinished, the name put out of my mind. When we ride away from here — '

'Just you,' Silva said. 'When *you* ride away from here. Pine's been disturbing the peace. Or maybe I can charge him with something more serious. All you need to know is when you ride out of town, he'll be taken in by my deputies. He'll spend time in jail. Oh, I hear what you're saying all right, but just because you tell me you're leaving doesn't mean I have to believe you. So remember this: if you do feel the urge to return to Cedar Creek, I've got Pine — and I've got your six-gun.'

'He's a Pinkerton man. You can't keep him locked up indefinitely without questions being asked.'

'You're in no position to tell me what I can or can't do. And my arm's already getting mighty tired, so you'd better come up with an answer I can believe, and fast.'

'My answer is action,' Gatlin said. 'I'm on my way.' He pushed himself to his feet, swayed as blood rushed to his head and he was engulfed by pain. It was agony bending to fix his bedroll. When he straightened for a second time, he thought he was about to vomit.

Then it was time to go. He exchanged blank looks with Charlie Pine, opened the door and stepped out into the corridor. And all the way down the stairs, across the entrance hall and out into the steady night rain, he could hear the murmur of voices from above and the occasional burst of coarse laughter.

5

By the time Gatlin had covered five miles the rain had stopped and the moon was gleaming fitfully through broken clouds. He was pointing the roan in a north-easterly direction, intent on putting just enough distance between himself and the town's limits to ensure his safety. It was his firm belief that Silva would not follow him, nor send riders to track his progress. And what Gatlin needed more than anything was a place to hole up, and time to think.

He blundered across the ideal spot after another ten minutes' stiff riding, the moonlight guiding him uphill through thick dark woods to an open mossy bank at the base of high cliffs, in those cliffs the narrow cleft marking the entrance to a dry cave. A few yards away, a stream of cold mountain water tumbled down through a rocky gully; he had everything he needed, and he was well away from any well-used trail.

Ten minutes later he had unsaddled and watered the roan and was sitting in bright moonlight at the cave's entrance, an almost smokeless fire crackling on the stone floor, both hands folded around a cup of hot coffee. The pain of bruises, a split lip and a battered nose were sharp reminders of the terrible beating he had suffered in the hotel room. As he looked out over the silent woods, his mind was occupied with Charlie Pine's predicament and the obstacles and dangers that lay ahead.

Today he had been forced to stand like a human punch bag while Jax Silva's deputy rained punishing blows on his unprotected head and body. But it was not over, it could not finish in that hotel room with flamboyant lawman Jax Silva calling the shots.

Next time, Gatlin vowed, it would be different. He had ridden in out of a wet night with high hopes, and seen them dashed in the heat of a violent assault. But today was not the end of his quest. Today, everything that happened in the Cedar Creek Hotel had marked a new beginning.

★ ★ ★

Sleep took him sooner than expected, the spell of concentrated thinking put off until the next morning. Bright sunlight streaming through the mouth of the cave woke him late, and he saw to the roan, gingerly swilled his bruised face in the waters of the tumbling creek then rebuilt the fire and cooked his breakfast.

Condensation was rising from the trees as the sun's heat dried the previous day's rain and, as he sipped his coffee and gazed at the thin mist, he let his mind range over problems and possibilities.

Cedar Creek lay to the south-west. From what Charlie Pine had told him, Gatlin calculated that the estate of several hundred acres owned by the man called Hood lay in the Big Horn foothills some miles beyond the town. The estate, Gatlin believed, had been bought with the proceeds of a train robbery for which he had spent eight years of a ten-year sentence in the Texas penitentiary. It had taken him a further twelve months to locate Hood. According to Pine, the big timber house where the man now lived was set back against dark Ponderosa pines and approached by a mile-long driveway, every yard of which could be kept under observation from the house's galleries and broad verandas.

Getting close to Hood without being seen by the men in his employ had always meant avoiding that driveway. Reaching Hood from any direction would be more difficult, Gatlin knew, now that he had stupidly trumpeted his arrival and come off second best in a bruising encounter with the law.

But that had been yesterday, those unfortunate incidents now deemed by a chastened Gatlin to be the new beginning. So, if that was true — what were his priorities?

He tossed away the coffee dregs, reached to the fire for the blackened coffee pot and refilled his cup.

Charlie Pine could look after himself. Silva would lock him in a strap-steel cell, but the operative would soon be missed by Pinkerton's Denver office. If Pine had left word where he was going, then Silva would soon be receiving a flood of increasingly insistent telegraph enquiries.

Of more concern to Gatlin was Pine's remark that he was only sixty per cent sure Hood was the man responsible for the train robbery. Sixty per cent was encouraging, but it left work to be done, enquiries to be made, people to talk to — and Gatlin was no longer free to ride into Cedar Creek.

All right, for a resourceful man, that was no insurmountable barrier: riding into town at night was inconvenient but, as he couldn't risk showing himself in daylight, he had no choice.

Unfortunately the lateness of the hour would again mean an almost empty street, many people abed, few ears to listen to his questions and a big risk of being spotted by an alert Jax Silva.

Gatlin put down his empty cup, dug out the makings and fashioned a smoke. He lit up, swore softly as he put the cigarette to his split lip and reluctantly tossed the unsmoked quirly into the dying fire.

And then he smiled.

Night time was the *right* time. He remembered the Wayfarer saloon, located at the top end of town. Where there were businesses, there would be back alleys. And if Gatlin wanted to dig for information, then who was the most likely man in any town to come up with the goods?

The saloonist. The aproned man who stood behind a bar listening in a deliberately bored manner to men with their tongues loosened by drink. That man's appearance was deceptive. He was never bored. He soaked up information, and he could keep his lip buttoned or talk freely — depending on the company.

And one thing Jim Gatlin had always prided himself on was his ability to get on with people, to soften them with his quiet charm. That talent had served him well during eight years behind bars, and it would serve him well again.

All he had to do was wait for darkness.

Sounded simple.

Trouble was, Jax Silva was holding Gatlin's pistol, his rifle had been stolen from its saddle boot on the way north from southern Texas, and Gatlin was about to go sneaking through the darkness to knock on the back door of a saloon.

Apart from a pocket knife with its blade blunted by years of use, Jim Gatlin was unarmed.

★ ★ ★

Gatlin lazed around for most of that day.

Late in the afternoon, to stretch the roan's legs, he saddled up and rode along the rocky open ground at the base of the cliffs. He pushed uphill, the roan's hoofs clattering on the stones, eventually emerging into bright sunlight above the tree-line. When he turned and sat easy in the saddle with his hands folded on the horn he could see the slopes of the Big Horn mountains to his right and, far below, the town of Cedar Creek. Main Street snaked down the hill between the business premises. The hotel was clearly visible at the bottom of the street, but from that distance Gatlin could see no sign of movement outside the jail.

Sight of the town again brought home to Gatlin the task he had set himself. He felt a flicker of self doubt, swore softly at his stupidity, and set off down the slope.

Back at the cave he cooked an evening meal, washed it down with

50

ice-cold water then prepared a pot of coffee. Smoke from the fire drifted into his face then on into the cave, and he narrowed his eyes. He poked with a stick, shifting the embers, then poured his coffee. It would be his last hot drink before setting off for town.

★   ★   ★

The sun had dropped behind the Big Horn mountains, the air had turned chill and heavy with dew. Gatlin was sitting at the mouth of the cave warming his hands by the fire's dying embers when the sound of hoofbeats came clearly to him through the trees. Close. Too close. Gatlin frowned. Although he knew Silva was unlikely to send men out to check on his movements, he had been keeping his ears tuned for unusual sounds ever since daybreak. Now, as the hoofbeats increased in intensity, he caught himself listening to determine which way the riders were heading.

51

South-west. They were riding *towards* Cedar Creek. And suddenly he caught a fleeting glimpse of them through the trees, three riders, cantering down the slope. There was an instant flood of relief as they rode on without pause. Then Gatlin resumed his listening, while mulling over what he had heard, and the implications.

The hoofbeats were fading rapidly as the riders pushed on towards town. Three horsemen, Gatlin mused. Not hurrying, but wasting no time. Not using the main trail into Cedar Creek.

Why should that bother him?

Because his own position was precarious. There was nothing sinister about riders choosing to approach Cedar Creek by a more difficult route — but still it stirred a worm of unease in Gatlin. There were too many possibilities, and not enough answers. Were they men who had ridden out of town early and passed below him unseen and unheard when he was still asleep? Had Silva sent Green and Mundt out to hunt him down? Were those two now returning to town to report their failure?

Or were the sounds he had heard made by strangers heading for town — and if so, who were they, and what was their business in Cedar Creek?

Yet even as those thoughts and others much more outlandish jostled for supremacy in his overheated mind, Gatlin was quick to banish them with a sudden, sheepish shake of the head.

What the hell was wrong with him? If it was the two deputies, Green and Mundt, he should thank his lucky stars they'd missed him and were heading back to town. If it was a bunch of strangers — well, new arrivals in town would attract attention, and *anything* that took Jax Silva's mind off Jim Gatlin was a welcome diversion.

Especially, Gatlin thought grimly, in about an hour's time when an unarmed man was hammering on the back door of the town's only saloon, an establishment that Jax Silva, if following the routine of a typical town lawman, would visit more than once in the course of an evening's duty.

Sombrely, Gatlin emptied the coffee pot over the fire. He went deeper into the cave, hesitated for a moment, then unbuckled the gunbelt with its empty holster and placed it with his bed roll. If nothing else, he had a base, a camp to which he could return.

Then he turned his back on his primitive retreat and went out into the cooling air to prepare the roan for another night ride.

6

'Out,' Jax Silva said.

The lock clicked. The door swung open. Charlie Pine rolled off the cot and walked out of the cell into the narrow corridor where a hanging oil lamp smoked.

He'd been in jail a couple of hours. The doctor had been called in to strap his injured hand. The skin around his right eye was turning purple.

'What happened?' Pine said. 'Someone out there carrying more weight than a small-town marshal?'

Silva sneered. 'Your whining wore me down.'

'Yeah,' Pine said, preceding the marshal through to the lamplit office. 'I'd say the whining you couldn't abide was the telegraph op warning you about the stream of wires from the Pinkerton's Denver office. Who was doing the

55

enquiring, my boss, Charlie Eames?'

Silva didn't answer. He slid behind the desk, found a printed form lying next to the typewriter, scrawled his signature.

'That's it. Your release form's signed, everything's official, all that's left is for you to get out of town.'

'There's the small matter of my gunbelt.'

'Over there, on the hook.'

'And Jim Gatlin's pistol.'

Silva looked up. 'That stays here.'

Pine grinned. 'Good idea. If I know the man he'll be back before long to collect it.'

'Get out of here,' Silva growled.

The rattle of hoofs turned both men's attention to the street. Pine collected his gunbelt and strolled to the open door. Three men were riding down the hill, their appearance difficult to make out in the dim street lighting. They drew rein across the street in front of the hotel, swung down, hitched their mounts and stamped across the plank walk to the front door.

Pine sensed Silva at his shoulder.

'More trouble?'

The marshal grunted.

'No reason to be. Men are free to come and go.'

'Jim Gatlin rides in out of the rain and it's trouble; three men ride in on a fine night, and you're happy.'

'Not unduly concerned,' Silva said. 'Gatlin's different. He spent eight years in the Texas pen.'

Across the street the last of the three men entered the hotel and shut the door. Silva returned to his desk. Pine heard the rasp of a match, caught the strong smell of cigar smoke.

'Not *unduly*. But concerned, nevertheless?'

'Tell you what,' Silva said. 'You're a Pinkerton man, why don't you wander over there, see what you can find out?'

For a moment, Charlie hesitated. What was this? Silva asking for his help? Then he nodded.

'Reckon I'll do that. I need a room,

anyway; I want to be here to watch the fun when Jim Gatlin rides back into town.'

★   ★   ★

It was full dark and raining again when Gatlin came down from the mountains and crossed the Cedar Creek town limits. The skies were heavy with clouds. There would be no moon that night.

He had donned his slicker as he emerged from the shelter of the woods onto the main trail. In appearance he was the same man who had ridden in some twenty-four hours earlier, but now he was battle-scarred, wiser, and with a clear objective. On the edge of town he moved the roan into a stand of trees and drew rein. From there, at the top of Main Street's long slope, he could look down to where the light from the street's hanging oil lamps spilled across the muddy wagon ruts and dimly illuminated the façades of

58

the business premises. But that was as far as the light reached. Blocked by the buildings themselves, it left the back alleys in darkness.

Exactly as expected; exactly the way he wanted it.

The front of the saloon was some fifty yards away. As he watched, a rider came up the street through a curtain of rain. He swung down, awkwardly tied his mount with the half-dozen other horses at the hitch rail. When he pushed open the doors and went into the saloon, the bandages on his right hand were bathed in light.

Charlie Pine.

Absently, Gatlin touched his split lip with his tongue, wondering what the hell to do. Pine was out of jail. Someone had tended to his injured hand. Gatlin would dearly have liked to hear the Pinkerton man's story, but his hands were tied: he could no more walk boldly after him into the saloon than he could show his face anywhere else in town.

Then it occurred to him that the more crowded the saloon, the less likely it was that sharp ears would hear him knocking at the back door. Or maybe, he mused, his knock would be heard by no one, and he would be forced to break in. And with that lingering and strangely exhilarating thought, he allowed himself a thin smile and got down to business.

With a soft clicking sound, Gatlin moved the roan out from under the trees.

He rode the horse at a slow walk towards the lamplit street, his gaze ranging ahead to the rutted slope, searching for any movement that might suggest Silva was on the prowl. He could see only as far as the general store and the bank. There, his view was cut off as the street turned to the right and plunged steeply.

Even so, that proved to be far enough.

As the wind gusted and he narrowed his eyes against the stinging rain, Gatlin saw a man walking up the plank walk on the saloon side of the street. No prizes for guessing his identity. Even in the dim light Gatlin could see the ivory butt of his gleaming six-gun and the tin badge of office glinting on a ridiculous cowhide vest, and the head ducked against the rain was wearing a white Stetson that was like a banner screaming the man's name and official standing.

With a soft curse and a shake of the head Gatlin tore his gaze away from the approaching lawman and cut sharp left so that he was hidden by the building closest to the edge of town. It was a ramshackle, tin-roofed affair that was probably a storeroom used by the saloonist. Gatlin moved the roan into the unlit area behind it. He was at the entrance to a wide alley-way he guessed ran the full length of Main Street. To his left a ravine cut away from town through a dense stand of aspen.

He'd reached his objective, and Jax Silva's arrival on the scene meant

Gatlin was now walking on thin ice. Suddenly, the lawman's half expected but definitely unwelcome presence was causing doubts to creep in. Despite his being in the alleyway *behind* the saloon and the bar room on the *other* side of the premises, Gatlin could hear the murmur of voices, the occasional burst of laughter. If he could hear sounds from the saloon, surely a man's hammering on the back door was unlikely to go unnoticed?

If he had intercepted Charlie Pine, the Pinkerton man could have created a mild diversion. Opened up a game of poker near the windows. Bought a drink for every man in the place.

Despite the dangers, Gatlin caught himself grinning. And the sudden good humour blew away the doubts and reminded him of the advantages of the noise he could hear. With luck, what he was about to do next would be drowned by the hubbub caused by good-humoured drinkers . . .

Gatlin dismounted, tied the roan to a

fence post on the far side of the alley, then splashed across to the rear of the saloon and flattened himself against the wall. Paint was peeling off a back door streaming with rainwater. The back room had a single window. Gatlin turned, peered in. The room was a kitchen with stove, pots and pans, lit by an oil lamp with the wick turned down. Incongruously, a gun rack holding several rifles was nailed to the far wall. An open door on the room's far side was an oblong of bright light. Gatlin could see the working side of a bar, one man with a patch over his eye sitting on the other side of the bar drinking from a tall glass, beyond him people moving and a pall of cigarette smoke hanging in the warm lamplight.

As he watched, the person tending bar moved into his field of view.

It was a woman. A buxom woman wearing a bright yellow dress, her brassy blonde hair held high with ornate combs.

Gatlin took a deep breath, closed his

eyes, counted to ten.

Then he bent down, found a wet stone, and tapped hard on the window.

Nothing happened. No reaction. The tapping was lost in the talk and the laughter.

Gatlin clenched his teeth and tried again, rapping harder, fully expecting the glass to shatter.

Suddenly the woman behind the bar appeared in the lighted doorway, looking intently towards the back window; looking directly at Gatlin's face.

Gatlin lifted a hand, and beckoned.

The doorway was restricting his view. One minute he could see movement, a person — then nothing. As he watched, the woman turned away and slipped out of sight. The man on the other side of the bar was looking in that direction. He appeared to be listening. Then he stepped down from the stool and he too walked out of Gatlin's field of view. Almost as quickly he reappeared. But now he was behind the bar.

The man, Gatlin guessed, had been told by the woman to take over as bartender. But where was *she*? What was she doing? A few seconds ago she appeared to have heard Gatlin knocking, seen his face at the window. But that might have been optimism obscuring the facts. In truth she could be taking her normal evening break — or, having seen Gatlin at the window, was even now warning Marshal Jax Silva about the man lurking in the alley.

Then, just when Gatlin was debating whether he should turn and run, she reappeared. The yellow dress sparkled with pearls and buttons. She was holding a shotgun in hands on which gold rings glittered. With the light from the bar room shining through the door and turning her blonde hair to a bright gold halo, she came across the dim kitchen. She stopped at the lamp, turned up the wick. The light illuminated a pleasant round face, blue eyes that were looking intently at Gatlin.

Sending a clear message to him she

cocked both the shotgun's hammers, shifted the weapon to her left hand and rested it against one padded hip. Then she walked the rest of the way, and unlocked the door.

7

In the Cedar Creek Hotel the gun-slinger named Wilson went to the window, lifted the curtain and looked out. The rain had eased, but the street was wet, the wagon ruts streaming. He couldn't see the livery barn where he and his companions had put their horses, but still the room was exactly where he'd wanted it: it overlooked the rainswept street, and he could see clear into the marshal's office.

Not that he expected trouble from the marshal of Cedar Creek, Wyoming. The man whose immediate superior was the Sheriff of Bighorn County was located too far north to have heard of Texas outlaws named Wilson, Hidalgo and River. And he'd have no reason to suspect newcomers looking for a night's shelter from the rain of any intent to commit a crime.

Which, Wilson knew, was a dangerous way to think. He knew the
marshal's name — Jax Silva — but
nothing more. Assuming the man
wearing the badge was a country boy
with straw in his hair was foolish. Best
to go in there with a good story, put it
on the table, watch the man's eyes. Like
playing a game of poker, but with the
stakes sky high . . .

Wilson was still looking thoughtfully
across the street when there was a
knock on the door. When he turned,
River and Hidalgo had walked in.

Hidalgo was a dark-eyed man with
the flowing moustaches of a Mexican
peasant and the demeanour of a bandit.
River was a wiry Texan with innocent
blue eyes. Wilson had got to know him
in a bar-room brawl when the Texan
had knifed a drunken lawman who'd
foolishly kept his badge tucked away in
his vest pocket. Wilson, ensconced at a
corner table with his back to the wall,
had used his six-gun as a club to batter
a way to the door, River back-pedalling

68

as he flourished the bloody knife to protect their backs.

River and Hidalgo were opposites in appearance, but thought like brothers. Wilson looked them over. He looked at their six-guns, butts shiny with use and tied down with rawhide thongs, and liked what he saw.

'You two settled in?'

'Sure.' River grinned at Hidalgo. 'One big room, next floor up. No Montezuma's palace, this, but better than sleeping under a tree.'

'Yeah, and this here's better than the cell I left a few weeks back,' Wilson said. 'Anyway, I don't plan on being here too long.'

River pursed his lips. 'Maybe. Or maybe it sounds too easy. All we've got is a name. Hood. Tomorrow we ask around, someone tells us where this feller lives, and we go see him and he opens this big safe — '

'In his bedroom,' Hidalgo said.

'According to the convict I shared a cell with,' Wilson said. 'He was in for cattle rustling, but ten years ago he was *part* of that train robbery I already mentioned. So he knows what he's talking about. He was there, he got paid, but he *knows* Hood kept the biggest share of that cash for himself.'

'Yeah, right, so it's in his bedroom,' River said impatiently. 'We go out there, he opens the safe and suddenly we're rich men and we ride south to where the sun's hot all damn year round.'

'The bank is just a little way up the hill,' Hidalgo said, 'but we turn our backs, ride out of town and rob a bedroom.'

'When are you going to stop complaining?' Wilson shook his head in mock despair. 'All right, it's not a bank. But looked at another way, what we're about to do is not a robbery. The money this man stole was heading for a string of banks. That meant it belonged to somebody else. Cattlemen. The owners of general stores, livery barns. Maybe it was your money, or my money. So what we're about to do can be seen as returning that cash to its rightful owners.'

River grinned. 'Yeah, except not one of us had any money in the first place.'

'So what *are* we going to do?' Hidalgo said. 'Take the cash from this man's bedroom and at last transport it to those banks who were expecting it ten years ago.' He flashed a grin. 'Beg your pardon, *señor*, we are so sorry it has taken us all this time . . . '

'Yeah, like hell we are,' Wilson said, and suddenly the tension broke and all three of them were laughing.

River reached behind his back and tossed a flat bottle of whiskey to Wilson. He uncorked it and took a long drink as River sat on the bed. The 'breed moved restlessly to the window.

Wilson tossed the bottle to River.

'This is what we do,' he said, and watched as Hidalgo turned away from the window, suddenly attentive.

'River, you said tomorrow we ask around, then ride out to Hood's place and he opens his safe and suddenly we're rich men. Maybe you're right, maybe it's not that easy. If a rich man sets up a bank in his house, he's going to employ one or two tough *hombres* to see his money stays in the safe.'

'No *problema*,' Hidalgo said. 'Wyoming *campesinos* up against three Texas *bandidos* — '

'No, not peasants. Unknown *gunmen*, always on the lookout for strangers acting suspicious,' Wilson said. 'We don't know those men, where they are or how good they are. We don't know for sure they're out there — and that makes it difficult.'

'So we ride out to Hood's place,' River said. 'Someone tries to stop us, you've found your guards.'

Wilson shook his head. 'Maybe that's the way it'll happen in the end. But first — and we're all agreed on this — first we've got to find Hood's place.' He looked speculatively at Hidalgo. 'You and River look too much like *bandidos*. With my good looks and pleasant manner I can charm the birds out of the trees. Tomorrow, I walk across the street and talk to the marshal.'

River frowned. 'Why not the general store? The saloon? Why don't we talk to the woman in the café when we eat breakfast? Going to the marshal is plain loco.'

'Not so. The best way of weighing up the opposition is meeting it face to face. Small-town marshal meets Texas outlaw — only that's not what he sees. I see what I'm up against, but all he sees is a visitor to his town passing the time of day.'

Hidalgo took the bottle from River, wiped the neck on his sleeve and drank. When he lowered the bottle his dark eyes were sceptical.

'We wish you every success,' he said to Wilson, 'but I think you are making one big mistake. This man Hood, he will have the town marshal in his pocket.'

'And that's not the half of it,' River said. 'The way I see it, this man Hood will have the whole damn *town* in his pocket — I reckon someone's been watching us from the time we rode down the hill and booked into this fleapit of a hotel.'

8

In the dim lamplight the shotgun was making Jim Gatlin sweat. The weapon was lying across the scrubbed board table. The hammers had been eased down onto the cartridges, but the blued barrels still bore the threat of instant death. The twin muzzles were black holes staring at Jim Gatlin; the triggers were within easy reach of the woman's soft, relaxed hands.

When she opened the back door she had used the shotgun to wave Gatlin into the room. She had rammed the muzzles hard into his ribs when he brushed too close to her with his cold, rain-wet slicker; then again when she sat him at the table and ordered him to talk fast — to talk his way out of a walk downhill to Silva's jail.

Gatlin had done that. He had reduced ten years of his life to less than ten minutes. All the time he was talking her blue eyes watched him intently, her gaze taking in his bruises, the shotgun maintaining a constant menace.

When Gatlin's story was nearing its close — when he reached the twelve months after he had been released from jail and for the first time mentioned the man named Hood in connection with all that had befallen him — he detected a change in those blue eyes. Hardness and scepticism faded. In their place he saw a growing acceptance of his story, and that slightly distant look that suggests interested speculation.

He had given her food for thought.

Abruptly, she slid the shotgun off the table and leaned it against the wall. Then she turned towards the door.

'Josh,' she yelled. 'Get in here.'

The man wearing the black eye-patch poked his head around the door.

'If Len's in tonight,' the woman said, 'get him to take over for a while. It's taken a long time to happen — but salvation just rode into town.'

* * *

Charlie Pine had found a table near a window overlooking Main Street and was sipping warm beer while the steam from his rain-soaked shirt rose to mix with the thick pall of cigarette smoke. The Pinkerton man had been sitting in the saloon for less than ten minutes, yet already he was fascinated by what he'd observed.

The woman behind the bar was a buxom blonde with limpid blue eyes and, Pine guessed, nerves of steel. But tonight she appeared distracted. A few minutes after Pine sat down she'd been disturbed by a noise in a back room. She'd peered through, then said something to a man with a black patch over his eye. He'd left his stool and started serving drinks. The woman had taken a shotgun from under the bar and gone into the back room.

She still hadn't reappeared.

Meanwhile, the flamboyant marshal, Jax Silva, had come in, dashing the rain from his white Stetson and sweeping the room with a searching gaze.

He'd spotted Charlie Pine, nodded, then gone over to the bar. He spoke to a tall, grey-haired man in a dark suit. The man turned, and his dark eyes looked across at Pine. He nodded slowly.

Silva had bought him a drink, then circulated, and seemed to be asking questions. But he'd got a such a cold reception from the man with the eye-patch that Charlie Pine couldn't suppress a smile of amusement.

He was still finding it difficult not to chuckle out loud when Silva came over to his table. The marshal was carrying a jolt glass of whiskey. He sat down, put his hat on the floor, ran fingers through his dark hair and tossed back the drink with a jerk of the wrist.

'Who's your friend?'

Silva shrugged. 'Tall feller? Haydn Crawford. Heads the town council.'

'For Hood?'

'Sometimes. But Haydn's his own man. If nothing's ruffling his feathers

78

he's fine, but he'll take just so much.' He cocked an eye at Pine. 'You get yourself a room in the hotel?' he said, putting down the glass.

'Number three, next to that bunch's leader. He's in the room you asked Gatlin to . . . vacate.'

Silva grinned. 'And?'

'The others are upstairs. They came down to talk. The walls are thin.'

'And those fellers're not shy.' Silva grinned. 'So, what's going on?'

'You'll get a visitor in the morning. Man named Wilson. He's going to ask questions about Hood.'

'And the others?'

'River and Hidalgo. They're on the next floor up. I got their names, but nothing else. Wilson got out of the Texas pen a couple of weeks ago. Seems he heard about Hood from a cattle rustler he shared a cell with. The man was part of a gang robbed the Atchison Topeka.' Pine sipped his beer, watched Silva. 'The gang was led by Hood. And I learned something else about him.'

79

'Go on.'

'He's keeps a safe at home. In his bedroom.'

'Banks get robbed,' Silva said, thoughtfully fingering his beard. 'All that tells me is Hood's playing safe — and that's not a pun.' He poked a finger in the empty glass, moved it around in a circle. When he looked up, his eyes were unreadable. 'That's more than I can say for your friend.'

'My friend?'

'Gatlin's back in town.'

Pine chuckled. 'What did I tell you? He's come back for that pistol bearing his initials.'

'He's looking in the wrong place, though I'm sure he'll get around to it,' Silva said. 'Right now he's talking to Kitty Mac in the back room.'

★ ★ ★

The place on the table once occupied by the shotgun was now filled by a bottle and three glasses. The oil lamp had been brought over, its wick now turned up to within a whisker of smoking so that its bright yellow light glinted on skin and eyes. The woman had got up to scrape a third chair close to the table. It was occupied by the man with the eye-patch, the cheekbones of an Indian, the strong mouth under a bushy moustache and the stained hat with its plaited leather band.

'This is Josh Notion,' the woman said. 'He's Cedar Creek's gunsmith. My name's Kitty Mac. If you ain't already guessed, I own this place.' Her glance at Notion was bitter. 'In this town, that's really something — right, Josh?'

The man nodded. He, too, had been examining Gatlin's bruised face and damaged lips. His eyes, too, had for a moment drifted towards distant speculation, only to come flashing back to life at the woman's remark.

'Kitty owns the saloon, I own my place. Considering the rest of the town's owned by Nathan Hood — yeah, I'd say we've got something to be proud of.'

'Owned by Hood — run by Hood?'

Notion shook his head. 'Oh no. Hood delegates, stays well out of it. Town council's run by a man called Haydn Crawford. He's well off, a decent enough man — but he's also averse to rocking the boat. He has an easy life. In five years nothing's happened to threaten that.'

'Until I arrived?'

Notion nodded. 'You aroused Kitty's interest as soon as you rode in — '

'But that was you looking out of the window?'

'Yeah — and you looked away fast when you spotted me.' Notion shrugged. 'So there you were, a lone rider. You interested Kitty, and then you interested me, but only because here in Cedar Creek you've been a topic of conversation for the past twelve months.'

'In case you ain't worked it out,' Kitty said, 'that's the day they unlocked the gates of the pen and let you walk free.'

'Why would that interest people?'

'When you had your day in court, you pointed the finger at Nathan Hood. That was a long time ago, but people have long memories. In these parts Hood's not what you'd call a popular man. So, news gets out of your release and folk around here can't wait to see what happens next.'

Notion cocked an amused eyebrow. 'Kitty's right, but the only reason I recognized you at all is because Silva had a bit of a game going, drawing moustaches and beards on old reward notices.'

'Oh, he's Gatlin all right,' Kitty Mac said, 'if you look under the bruises. And the tale he tells is a mite different to the one Silva's been spreading around.'

'Sounds like Silva's making some kind of vendetta out of this,' Gatlin said.

'He looks after Hood's interests. Has to,' Kitty said, 'or he'd be out of a job.

And looking after Hood's interests means keeping troublemakers like you away from the big man.'

'With the help of those two deputies, Green and Mundt?'

Notion shook his head. 'Lane Green and Gus Mundt are Hood's men — though that doesn't make them loyal employees. Like most people associated with Hood they're in it for the money. If things go wrong . . . ' He looked at Gatlin's face. 'I'd guess Green was the one used his fists to alter your appearance.'

'He did that, and deliberately broke a man's hand. Set up and presided over by Silva.'

'Let me guess: the injured man's the young feller who's been asking questions around town.'

'Charlie Pine. A friend of mine working out of the Pinkerton's Denver office.'

'Is he now?' Notion said. 'And he's the one led you to Hood — right?'

He noted Gatlin's nod of acquiescence, then looked at the woman. 'Go on, Kitty, spill it — what's this about a different story?'

Kitty Mac cut Gatlin's ten-minute tale down to five, but before she was a dozen words in Notion's eyes had hardened. When the woman was done, he shook his head in wonderment.

'Nathan Hood,' he told Gatlin, 'is a businessman who made his money investing in the California gold fields and moved north to buy a town.'

'That's his story. What do they say about me?'

'Ten years ago you led the gang that cut down a tree to stop an Atchison Topeka train and got away with a fortune in cash.'

Gatlin grunted. 'I can't blame you for believing stories you've been fed. But if you're prepared to believe me, you know the names have been switched around. Hood is from Texas. He was behind that Atchison Topeka robbery. I was running a small family ranch. For some reason it was my name got plucked out of a hat, and I was framed.

I did eight years in the pen for another man's crime.'

'Which means Hood invested stolen money,' Notion said. 'That was clever. When the proceeds came flooding in, the money was clean and Hood was in the clear.'

The bottle clinked against glass as Kitty Mac freshened the drinks.

'So now we know why Hood started worrying about grey hairs the day you walked out of jail. If you open your mouth here you could blow his comfortable life apart.' She looked hard at Gatlin. 'What we don't know is why it was you he framed.'

'That's one of the questions I intend asking when I meet the man,' Gatlin said.

'The question bothering me,' Notion said, 'is what your other intentions are when you do meet him.'

'I don't know.'

'Tell him who you are, then kill him for what he did to you?'

'I told you, I don't know. For so long

I've had this vision in my mind: me, walking up to the man called Hood, confronting him — but that's as far as it goes; I can't see any further.'

Gatlin paused. He had been observing Kitty Mac and Notion as they listened to his story, and seen the surge of interest in their eyes as he told of Hood's criminal past. The inference was clear: for years they had been desperate to get rid of Hood, and Gatlin's unexpected arrival in Cedar Creek with astonishing news had turned vague hope into a possibility. Not yet a certainty, but . . .

'What about you two?' Gatlin said. 'You own your businesses, yet I can see you sniffing the air like hounds scenting helpless prey.'

'Johnson over at the general store pays rent to Hood. So does Millie — she runs the café — and Stan Purvis down at the hotel. Took 'em years to build those businesses, but they were bought out for peanuts.'

'All right. We're all on the same side,

but knowing something is not the same as proving it and then getting close enough to Hood to shove it in his face.'

Kitty Mac frowned at that. Then she turned her head to listen, and seemed to find something disturbing about the noise — or lack of it — in the other room. Stern-faced, she heaved herself out of the chair and went through to the bar.

Notion finished his drink, then settled back to roll a smoke.

Gatlin sat pondering. He'd set a few facts straight, listened with mixed feelings to those thrown back at him by Kitty Mac and Notion. Hood had the town sewn up. The marshal was in his pocket. He employed hard men. Nothing unexpected, but having his fears confirmed didn't make it any easier for Gatlin.

'Maybe,' he said, 'I could get close to Hood on a day he rides into town. What's he use, a top buggy? Easy to spot, I could stop him out in open country.'

'Bright ideas are always the first to get knocked back,' Notion said. 'Hood stopped coming to town. I can't recall seeing the man in, oh, I don't know, more than a year, though a couple of the cowpokes who're always riding past the spread have seen him as recently as last week.'

'So if he doesn't come to town, how does he manage his business affairs?'

'Through his daughter, Belinda. She visits the bank at least once every week.' Notion ran his tongue along the cigarette paper and looked at Gatlin from under his eyebrows. 'And don't you go thinking what I think you're thinking.'

'Get at the man through his daughter?'

'She's a fine woman. I reckon she's in her early twenties, so she'd have been ten or thereabouts when that train was robbed. You ask me, I'd say she knows nothing about her pa's . . . past misdemeanours — '

Suddenly he broke off and twisted in

his chair, the cigarette forgotten. A muted argument had broken out in the bar shortly after Kitty Mac had gone through. Without Notion or Gatlin noticing, that war of words had gone from a gentle simmer to boiling point. Now it was boiling over. A man was shouting hard enough to rattle bottles, Kitty Mac's shrill voice risked shattering glass as she lashed out in reply. And suddenly the vociferous altercation increased in volume.

'Jax Silva,' Notion said, 'and I reckon he's using his badge of authority to force his way in here. You'd best get out, and fast — '

Again he was interrupted. This time it was from the alley. A boot hit the back door. It crashed open. Lane Green slipped in out of the rain and stepped to one side. He held a cocked six-gun in his gloved hands. His eyes, as they focused on Gatlin, were alight and seething with malice.

Then Kitty Mac came backing out of the bar. She swung to face Notion as the white Stetson and dark-bearded countenance of Jax Silva loomed behind her. In one raking glance she saw Notion half out of his chair, rain drifting in through the open back door, the six-gun in Lane Green's hand.

'No!' she screamed.

She was too late to stop Notion. He flung himself sideways out of the chair, then lunged at Green. He went in low, wrapped his arms around the gunman's waist and slammed him back against the window sill. Green's head whipped back, cracked against the glass. Then he snarled, lifted the six-gun and brought it down hard on Notion's head.

The crack was sickening. The gunsmith groaned and sank to his knees.

Kitty Mac's face was white. Incredibly nimble despite her weight, she darted across the room. Her hands were outstretched, her eyes on the shotgun propped against the wall. She reached it before anyone moved, swung with it clutched in her big hands.

But Gatlin had cause to remember

Lane Green's ruthless streak. As the gunman grinned and brought his six-gun to bear on the blonde saloonist, as Jax Silva flipped out his ornate pistol and thumbed back the hammer, Gatlin stepped behind Kitty Mac and enfolded her ample body in a protective embrace.

'Leave it be,' he whispered, close to her ear. 'There'll be another time, another place.'

Kitty tensed. Gatlin could smell scented powder, warm, heady perfume, and the perspiration of anger and fear. Then she relaxed in his arms and lowered the shotgun.

Silva beamed at Gatlin.

'Nice work, feller — but one good deed never was enough to keep a stupid man out of jail.

9

Jim Gatlin's only experience of jail had come in the long days prior to his trial and incarceration in the Texas state penitentiary. It had been nothing like this.

Ten minutes ago Josh Notion had recovered from the pistol whipping and volunteered to take care of Gatlin's horse. Silva and his prisoner had walked down the hill in the rain. Now Gatlin was sitting on a chair in Jax Silva's office drinking hot coffee, the lawman was in the swivel chair behind his desk, white Stetson discarded, a steaming tin cup in his hand. The door was open. The heavy rain had ceased, the night air was cool and clean and the streaming wagon ruts glinted in bright moonlight.

The only intimation to Gatlin that he was a prisoner, and not free to walk out through that open door, was the fancy six-gun lying on Silva's desk. It was within easy reach of the lawman's right hand, and pointed in Gatlin's direction.

Silva's next words were equally pointed.

'I don't want you to get too cosy over there. A cell's where you're headed; a cell's where you'll spend the night — at the very least. But I'm a reasonable man. If a man I arrest's got a story to tell, I'm willing to listen.'

'This is after you've had him softened up?'

'Son, nothing's ever as simple as it looks on the surface. You're carrying an old sack bearing the Atchison Topeka name. I know you've got unfinished business with Hood, who just happens to be my boss. So why don't you help me out here before I tuck you up in bed? Fill in some of the gaps for a mighty puzzled lawman.'

What the hell, Gatlin thought. He took a deep breath, followed Kitty

Mac's lead and cut his story down to five minutes' brisk talking. While he spoke, the marshal sipped his coffee, stroked his beard, teased the long hair at the nape of his neck — and all the while the cynical grey eyes never left Gatlin.

When Gatlin drew to the end of his tale, Silva nodded slowly, thoughtfully.

'Told real well. Trouble is, I'm supposed to believe a story that goes dead against everything I've been hearin' for the past several years. To compound my puzzlement, that Pinkerton pardner of yours gave me more disturbing news that seems to back up your story.'

'I'm amazed you let him go, more amazed he'd give you the time of day.'

'Lettin' him go was a favour to Charlie Eames over in the Pinkerton's Denver office. What Pine gave me was that favour returned.'

'And amounted to?'

'Take a look over at the hotel.'

Gatlin turned in his chair. Through the doorway he could see across the street, most of the hotel's front. Light showed in three of the upstairs rooms.

'One of those,' Silva said as Gatlin turned back, 'is occupied by the Pinkerton man.'

'And next to it?'

'Your old room? That's now occupied by one of the three night riders: Wilson. The other two, River and Hidalgo, are in the room above. They've all got loud voices. Pine tells me those walls are like paper.' He waited, smiled crookedly. 'I was kind of hoping, you being one of Texas's ex-convicts, a couple of those names would ring a few bells.'

'Just the one: Wilson.'

'You know him?'

'Know of him. He shared a cell with a man who always looked at me kind of leery — Christ knows why.'

'Maybe he knew something you didn't, and he was keepin' it from you but passing it to Wilson,' Silva said. 'Maybe that's why it took you a year to reach Cedar Creek, while this Wilson managed it in just a few weeks

96

— according to your pal Pine.'

Gatlin nodded. 'So now what? You've got two different versions of the same story. You've got three men across the street about to do . . . what?'

'Wilson's coming to see me in the morning. The name of Hood will be prominent in the conversation.'

'And me?'

'I've been pondering on that one. Oh, you'll spend the night in jail. Best place anyway, them being over there and you and them on some kind of a collision course over Hood. That takes us to tomorrow.'

Silva sipped his coffee, put down the cup and sucked his teeth. 'Tomorrow, when Wilson crosses the street, if I leave the door to the cell block open and you've got sharp ears . . . '

'If I haven't got them now,' Gatlin said, grinning, 'I'll grow them over-night.'

★   ★   ★

It was long past midnight. The doors had swung to behind the last of the drinkers. The oil lamps in the bar had been blown out, and in the gloom the air was hot and smoky.

In the back room, the lamp that had guided Jim Gatlin to the back door had again been lowered. The back door, its latch shattered by Green's kick, was kept closed by a wooden wedge rammed under its rotting lower edge.

Kitty Mac and Josh Notion were sitting at the table. No whiskey, this late. Instead there was hot coffee, and the pot was burbling soothingly on the black iron stove.

'How's your head?'

Josh grinned wryly. 'Still in one painful piece.'

'Quite a couple of days, we've had. Gatlin hits town. We talk to him, get tangled up with Silva and Lane Green, now Gatlin's back in jail. Where does that leave us?'

'Exactly where we were before he rode in. Hood still owns most of the town. He doesn't own us. If we're content to leave it like that . . . '

'And Gatlin?'

Notion shrugged, winced as the move jolted his head and scattered his thoughts.

'Gatlin makes a difference,' he said, choosing his words. 'If we believe his story, he was innocent of any crime but spent eight years in the pen. He turned up in Cedar Creek chasing the man who framed him. With nowhere to go, hungry for information, he came to us. We listened, all three of us talked some — but now he's back in a cell.'

'He makes a difference,' Kitty said, chewing over the words, brow furrowed in concentration, 'because resolving his problem helps this town. If Hood gets his comeuppance, he goes to jail. If he goes to jail, ownership of the businesses he bought out reverts to the original owners.'

'Or Belinda takes over.'

'She can't do that. The owners were bought out with stolen money.'

'So now it gets complicated.' Notion sipped the hot coffee, pursed his lips thoughtfully. 'If the money was stolen, it has to be paid back. But that money's been spent. So where does that leave Millie over at the café? Or old Stan Purvis, struggling to keep the hotel running? In debt — or worse?'

'Here's another complication,' Kitty said. 'Word in the bar was that three night riders have taken a room in Stan's hotel. What's *their* game?'

'And who would know?'

'Silva?' She thought for a moment, then said, 'Speaking of Silva, that Pinkerton man with the injured hand was in the bar, talking to him. Considering what Silva had done, there was very little sign of friction — so what was going on?'

Josh shrugged. 'I can find out. That, and more. Yesterday, when Gatlin rode in, I said I'd stroll down to the jail. I never got around to it. Maybe I should.'

'No time like the present.'

'You're right. The night air will clear my head.'

'And the talk with Jax Silva,' Kitty said, 'could clear the air.'

★   ★   ★

The night was cool and clear, the street drying in a light breeze, the countless stars a brilliant canopy dimming the town's oil lamps. The thickly wooded slopes on both sides of Cedar Creek were black against the luminous night skies. By the time Josh Notion reached the jail the pleasurable stroll had caused him to forget the pain of each jolting footstep and reduced the knotty problems taxing his brain to mere passing irritations. Jim Gatlin's arrival in town was a storm blowing in to rock whatever boat Hood was sailing in. The damage was irreversible. Nothing would ever be the same again.

Notion pushed open the jail's door and walked in. Marshal Jax Silva started. He was dozing in his chair, his booted ankles crossed on the desk next to the typewriter. He opened one eye, saw Notion, opened the other, yawned and swung his feet to the floor with a thump.

'If you're here to press charges against Lane Green, forget it. You do that and I'll have you for harbouring a fugitive.'

'Fugitive from what? The man's served his time, and done no wrong in this town.'

'He's in a cell right now, I reckon we can soon cook something up to keep him in a while longer.'

'You and Hood?'

Suddenly Silva's eyes were guarded. He gestured to a chair, and watched as Notion sat down.

'So. If you're not after getting even with Green — what's this about?'

'This and that. A Pinkerton man who's been poking around. Jim Gatlin's arrival — as expected. Three strangers who booked into the hotel — unexpectedly, yet I'll eat my hat if their arrival here's not connected to Hood's troubles.'

'Hood's a rich man. This is the first I knew he *had* any troubles.'

'That's bull, Silva. He's been expecting trouble ever since Gatlin got out of the pen. Ten years ago Gatlin was suspected of robbing the Atchison Topeka and he went on the run. He was caught a year later. At his trial, Gatlin fingered Hood as the man who was framing him. The evidence was against him, and the judge wouldn't listen. Gatlin served eight years. He got out twelve months ago. Since then, Hood's been watching his back.'

'You're not listening, Notion. Hood's rich: when trouble comes along, a rich man pays someone to make it disappear.'

'You?'

Silva shrugged.

'What about the Pinkerton man?'

'Charlie Pine? What about him?'

'Hounding Jim Gatlin carries no risk. But Pine's got the backing of a massive organization. By assaulting him you've bought trouble — for yourself and, indirectly, for Hood.'

'Forget Pine. Me and him have reached an understanding.' Silva waved a dismissive hand. 'It's getting late, Notion. What exactly did you call in for? You said 'this and that', but how about getting to the point so we can all get some shuteye?'

Notion hesitated. Why *had* he walked down the hill? Because he wanted to know what the hell was going on. Maybe he'd hoped to find Silva changed in some way; thrown off balance by events running out of his control, his unswerving allegiance to Hood weakened by the possibility that the powerful man's reign could be coming to an end . . .

'In Cedar Creek,' Notion said, 'everything starts and ends with Nathan Hood. I suppose I came down here to ask how the past couple of days are affecting him. Because he's finished, isn't he? Jim Gatlin's the kiss of death. Today, tomorrow . . . sooner or later

. . . Cedar Creek is going to see the back of Nathan Hood.'

Jax Silva climbed to his feet, stretched, grinned.

'I've got empty cells out back, and every one of 'em's furnished with a cot and a corn husk mattress. I can take my pick, and that's where I'm going to sleep the rest of the night away. But before I do — before you walk back up the hill — get this into your head: you've got it all wrong. Everything is under control, in town, out of town. Nothing, and I mean *nothing* that's happened in the past year, has had the slightest effect on Nathan Hood.'

PART TWO

10

The harsh low light of early morning streamed in through the trees, softened by the mist lingering over the rolling green pastures of the estate known as Tall Timbers. As she emerged from the white house with its wide balconies and terraces and paused to gaze across the dew-soaked grounds, the tenseness across Belinda Hood's shoulders seemed to melt away. It was always the same. No matter how overwrought she might be — and she'd been mad enough to tear paper for most of the past twelve months — the green acres surrounding the house always acted as a balm to soothe body and soul. Today, with that calm, there came a conviction: any suggestion that her home was being put at risk by the arrival in Cedar Creek of a convicted thief was, well, preposterous. Her father had bought the land, built the house, nurtured the estate as it matured. He had done it legally, with the returns from money he had invested in gold.

Tall Timbers had been her home for almost ten years. It would always be her home.

With confidence bolstered and her mind at peace, Belinda moved away from the shadow of the house and into the strengthening sunlight. Two minutes later the black top-buggy, driven by Lane Green, came rumbling around the house from the stable yard. Belinda handed up her briefcase and climbed aboard. Green waited until she had settled in the seat, then clicked the horse into motion and they set off down the drive.

Behind them rode Gus Mundt. Armed escort, Belinda thought. With Green by my side and Mundt following on behind, *nobody* can touch us. Yet even as those thoughts reassured her she experienced the pang of uneasiness that always hit her when she was near these two men, thought about them;

about the cold ruthlessness of the one, the coarseness of the other . . . their unbending loyalty to her her father that she knew had never truly been put to the test.

They'd covered fifty yards when a clear shout rang out. Belinda touched Green's arm and twisted in her seat to look back at the house. The front door was open. The man standing in the opening — tall, the sunlight glinting on dark hair touched with grey — lifted his hand in a wave.

Belinda smiled. Returned the wave. Watched the man turn away and the door close.

Then she faced front and settled herself — briefcase in her lap — as Green flicked the reins and the top-buggy rolled down the long drive and on towards Cedar Creek.

★   ★   ★

The first impression Wilson got was of a fancy pants too fond of his appearance

111

to be of much use as a Western lawman. A second longer glance told him forcefully that the first impression was wrong. Marshal Jax Silva's eyes had alighted on him the moment he kicked the mud from his boots and stepped through the door, watched him as he walked across the office to stand by the desk, and without effort weighed up the visitor and dumped him in the category labelled worthless drifter.

Or so it seemed to the impressed gunslinger. And this, he told himself, was before the small-town lawman had opened his goddamn mouth.

He glanced at the open doorway leading, he supposed, to the cell block, dismissed that disturbing thought from his mind, and met the marshal's enquiring gaze.

'Figured I'd beat you to the punch.'

Silva was standing tall and straight as he clattered an empty coffee pot onto a shelf over the stove.

'You'd need to get up a mite earlier in the day to do that, Wilson. I watched you and your pards ride in, saw you book into the hotel. I can even tell you what time the lamp was blown out in room number two.'

'It never was, as far as I recall.'

'Then we agree on something,' Silva said, and the grey eyes were amused. 'Sit down. I'll listen for five minutes, because I always did like a good story.' He looked sideways at Wilson. 'After that I've got a prisoner to feed. Tough customer — or thinks he is. An ex-con called Jim Gatlin.'

Wilson dropped into a chair, striving to hide the effect of twin shocks that had hit him like buckets of cold water. The marshal knew his name — but how could that be? And Jim Gatlin — *here*, in Cedar Creek?

'You knowing Gatlin,' Silva said mildly, 'saves time, because it tells me a lot about you without the need for questions.'

He folded his long frame into the chair behind the desk, sat back and waited.

'Gatlin?' Wilson shook his head. 'Can't say that name rings a bell.'

'Pull the other one. Your eyes give you away, son.'

'Help me out, here. Where's this Gatlin from?'

'Texas state pen, the same as you.' Silva reached out a hand, banged the typewriter carriage sideways and the bell pinged. 'Everybody knows why Gatlin's in town. What's your story?'

'I'm looking up an old friend. We lost touch after the war.'

'That'd be Nathan Hood. Only I don't see him as an old friend.' Silva watched Wilson's eyes, nodded. 'You get out of the pen a few of weeks ago, next thing you're in Cedar Creek looking for this feller you lost touch with — who happens to be just about the richest man in these parts.'

Wilson teetered the chair back on two legs, rocked gently.

'Now that is a surprise,' he said, wondering where the hell the marshal was getting his information. 'Old Nate's

114

done real well for himself.'

Silva snorted.

'Give me credit for having a scrap of intelligence,' he said. 'You're trying to locate Nathan Hood because a cattle rustler you shared a cell with helped rob the Atchison Topeka. He told you Hood's got a heap of cash in a safe he installed in his house.'

'In his bedroom,' Wilson said, and suddenly his grin had turned nasty.

'Ah. So now it's cards on the table and a change of story.'

Wilson sneered. 'All that tells you is I was in the pen with a mouthy cattle rustler. You already *know* that.'

Silva reached for a sack of Bull Durham, his eyes thoughtful. He opened the sack, patted his pockets for papers, looked across at Wilson.

'For a minute there, son, I thought you were about to come clean. Seems you ain't, so here's where I spike your guns — beat *you* to the punch. I know you and your owlhoot partners are in town to rob Nathan Hood. That's a fact. And here's another for you to chew on: you'll never make it.'

'Well, I've got to tell you the opposition scares the hell out of me,' Wilson said. 'There's a fancy-Dan settin' behind his desk wearing a tin badge, and I've heard tell of an old deputy called Ned Riley who's usually too sick to turn in.'

And then he stopped, blinked.

He was staring into the muzzle of a cocked six-gun that had appeared out of nowhere.

'The reason you'll never make it,' Silva said, as if there had been no interruption to his steady flow of words, 'is because your pards will be across the street in the hotel and you'll be over here looking at the wrong side of strap-steel bars and wondering what the hell's happened. On your feet, son. There's a suite of rooms out back I reserve 'specially for visitors like you.'

★ ★ ★

In the cell across the passageway, the man called Wilson was lying on his back on the cot, smoking a cigarette. His eyes were closed. Occasionally the cigarette trembled in his fingers.

Watching him, Jim Gatlin reckoned — hoped — he was more than half asleep.

'So,' Charlie Pine said, 'are you going to tell me what happened last night?'

He was in Gatlin's cell, sitting cross-legged on the end of the cot, his injured hand in his lap. He'd just been telling Gatlin how, after breakfast, he'd been watching from the window of room three in the Cedar Creek hotel as Wilson entered the jail. The man had not come out again. Interested, keen to talk to Gatlin, Pine had strolled across the street. Marshal Jax Silva had agreed to a ten-minute visit, opened Gatlin's cell and grinned like a cat who's got the cream as he locked the two men in.

Now, swiftly and in a quiet voice, Gatlin related the events in the saloon's back room. He told the Pinkerton man about Green bursting in through the back door, how the gunslinger had downed Josh Notion with a vicious blow from his six-gun, about his own necessary but pleasurable restraining of the buxom Kitty Mac followed by his arrest and subsequent talk with Silva before the marshal locked him in the cell for the night.

'Silva told me you'd been doing some eavesdropping for him over at the hotel,' he finished. 'And that what you heard sort of backed up my story.'

'That's right,' Pine said. 'Seems the feller sharing a cell with Wilson was in on that train robbery. Knows all about Hood. I passed on the information to Silva in the saloon before he barged through to arrest you.'

'Damn!' Gatlin swore softly, cursing what screamed of a missed opportunity. 'That cattle rustler was there in the pen, as close to me as Wilson is now, all I had to do was *talk* to him . . . '

Pine glanced across the passage as Wilson stirred, settled. He leaned forward to look toward the door leading to the front office. It was still closed. Then he spoke to Gatlin in a conspiratorial murmur.

'Too late for cryin' over what might have been,' he said. 'What we've got to set our minds to now is gettin' you out of here.'

'Silva won't agree to that. He's paid to look after Hood, and he's already halfway to getting this bit of bother sorted out. He's got me; he's got Wilson. My guess is he'll keep us locked up while he goes after the other two.'

'Giving him a hand of four aces to show Hood.' Pine grimaced. 'I don't think it's as easy as you make out. Far as I know the only help Silva's got comes from an old-timer, Ned Riley.'

'Then he'll walk out in the street, swear in the first two men he sees.'

Pine shook his head. 'Something tells me he won't do that. The man thinks a heap of himself. He'll want to go it alone, come out of it the shiny hero on the big white horse.'

Gatlin thought for a moment. 'A lot depends on those two across the street . . . River, Hidalgo? They'll realize soon enough Silva's got Wilson locked in a cell. That'll throw them — but only for a while. And we both know the type. They'll start calculating the odds. Do they cross the street with guns blazing and bust Wilson out of jail? Or do they leave him to rot, go after Hood's cash and split it two ways instead of three?'

Pine said, 'If I was a betting man . . .'

'I *do* think you're right about Silva,' Gatlin went on. 'And if he is going to play the hero, he'll choose the best time. The best time is after dark. And you've seen the inside of that hotel. The only way out of room two is along the passage and down those stairs, or out the window. My guess is he'll station Ned Riley in the street. Even the old-timer could handle that chore, with a shotgun. Silva will go in the front way himself.'

'If he does that,' Pine said, speculatively, 'is he forced to leave the jail undefended?'

Gatlin shot him a glance, saw where Pine's thoughts were heading, and shrugged.

He didn't know the answer to that, but one thing was certain: unless he was prepared to waste a whole year's searching, he *had* to get out of jail. And he'd done some thinking overnight. The eight cruel years he'd languished in the penitentiary when he was innocent of any crime could *not* be thrown away, but now his dogged pursuit of Nathan Hood had met with complications. Three outlaws were after Hood's money, whereas Gatlin wanted . . . hell, he was no longer sure *what* it was he wanted.

The truth?

The truth was he'd been framed by the man who carried out the Atchison Topeka robbery, and he supposed what he wanted most of all was to look that man in the eye. But his thinking had gone no further. He had already said as much to Josh Notion: he had no idea what he was going to do when he came face to face with Nathan Hood — but there was only one way that question could be answered.

'If we're both right, busting out of here looks easy. But I never did like relying on ifs.'

Pine pulled a face. 'You worry too much. I'll have our horses in the alley. When Silva crosses that street, I walk in and unlock the cell and we both walk out the back door.'

'Maybe. But you've got all day to think about it. What I want you to do while you're passing the time is go talk to Josh Notion.'

'Why?'

'Just talk. Him and Kitty Mac are knowledgeable, and they made a stand against Hood. Ask their opinion. Hell, see if they want to help. We don't know Silva; we're guessing his reactions to a given situation — and we could too easily be wrong.'

And then another voice broke in.

'Mister, you can't *afford* to be wrong.'

Gatlin looked at Pine — then snapped his gaze to the other cell. Wilson was up on one elbow, grinning across at them.

'I sleep light, and I've got sharp ears and, the way you tell it, what I've been listening to seems like an easy way out of here.'

'For me, not you,' Gatlin said.

'Oh no,' Wilson said, and now the grin had slipped. 'See, it only needs one loud holler from me at the wrong time, and you're finished. So it's down to this: you go, and I hang on to your shirt-tails — and if you don't like the sound of that then, believe me, for you it ain't going to happen.'

11

It was still only mid-morning when Charlie Pine crossed the street from the jail, walked the few yards down to the premises standing between the café and the livery stables and opened the door to let the bright sunlight flood into Josh Notion's gun emporium. Immediately the Pinkerton man thought, wrong word: this was no fast-turnover shop selling cheap .22 rifles to old ladies planning to shoot squirrels or jack rabbits, but a craftsman's business owned by a man who loved high quality weapons. The small room was rich with the smell of thin oil, gunpowder, metal filings. In a glass case on the back wall flintlock rifles dating back to the Mexican-American war glistened on felt-lined wooden racks, flanked by the latest fast-action, magazine-loading Winchesters and Remingtons.

Notion was behind the counter, a

metal file in his hands as he focused his good right eye on a rectangle of metal clamped in a small vice.

He looked up when Pine walked in.

'Let me guess,' he said. 'A Pinkerton man never sleeps, so you've come up with more questions to keep other folk awake nights.'

'Try again.'

The gunsmith wiped his hands on an oily rag, and cocked his head.

'Jim Gatlin sent you over. He wants me to bust him out of jail.'

'You, or Kitty Mac,' Pine said, and waited.

'I take it you're joking?'

'Maybe, maybe not. Gatlin wants out, and we do have a makeshift sort of plan, but — '

'Outside the law?'

'Has to be. The law put him in there, in the shape of Jax Silva.'

'Yeah. Well, Silva's stubborn. There's a good lawyer in town. He could get Gatlin out, but it might take time.'

'Time's something Gatlin's short of.'

Pine hesitated. 'You know about the three men who booked into the hotel?'

'Kitty heard rumours. And I know Silva's got one of 'em in jail.'

'The one dozing in a cell is Wilson. He's a couple of weeks out of the Texas pen. They're all here after Hood's money. The others are River and Hidalgo.'

For a few moments there was silence. Pine rested a hip against the counter and ran his eyes over the displayed weapons. Notion fiddled with metalworking tools on the low shelf behind the counter, then wiped his hands again and tossed the rag into a waste bin.

'Come on,' he said, 'let's you and me take a walk.'

He donned his hat with the plaited leather band and led Pine up the hill at a fast pace, a broad-shouldered man of middle age who was still breathing slowly and evenly when he and his companion left the sunlight for the dim, cool interior of the saloon. The big room was empty of customers. Kitty

Mac was behind the bar, writing in a ledger. Strands of blonde hair strayed becomingly from the tortoiseshell combs.

Wiping the pen's nib on a cloth and pushing the stopper into the bottle of ink, she watched the two men traipse through the thin sawdust.

'Here comes trouble,' she said. 'This used to be a quiet town. There's more happened here in the last couple of days . . . '

'We'll talk out back,' Notion said and walked around the bar.

Pine followed. Kitty winked at him as he passed, then tagged along behind. She left the dividing door open so she could hear if a customer walked in, and they gathered around the table.

'We're honoured,' Notion told Kitty. 'This big-time Pinkerton man's come begging for help.'

'Or ideas,' Pine said, smiling. 'You've taken quite a shine to Jim Gatlin since he rode in, so . . . '

'Let's just say he's livened up the place,' Kitty said drily, 'when it was dying a slow, Hood-induced death.'

Notion chuckled. 'I like that.'

'Yes, but there's more to it,' Pine said. 'Through the aforementioned Hood, your lives are linked to Gatlin. What he does affects you two.'

'Or what he doesn't do,' Kitty said, suddenly sober. 'And where he is now, he can't do much.'

'That's about it,' Pine said — and waited.

After a brief silence, Notion said, 'Where do you fit in? How does an ex-con get a Pinkerton operative on his side?'

'We're distant cousins, both from Texas. I joined the Pinkertons a year after Jim was convicted. It was natural he should come to me when he was released, and wanted to find Hood.'

'All right.' Notion nodded his acceptance. 'What's this makeshift sort of a plan you were being cagey about?'

'It stands or falls on a hypothesis.'

'So does this saloon,' Kitty said, straight-faced. 'The bank finances me on the assumption people like you are going to buy drinks.'

'Later,' Pine said absently, wondering how to expand on what he'd said. Then he shrugged.

'Silva's looking after Hood's interests. He's got Gatlin and an outlaw called Wilson in jail. We figure he'll move on the other two, River and Hidalgo, after dark. With him and Ned Riley fully occupied at the hotel, that'll leave the jail unprotected for anything from a couple of minutes to half an hour. I'll have horses waiting in the back alley . . . '

He watched Notion and Kitty Mac exchange glances. Saw Notion cock a questioning eyebrow and Kitty pull a face and spread her hands palm up.

'If Silva's been reading your notes, it should work,' Notion said. 'On the other hand, he might have read your notes and thought, to hell with it, I'll do things my way — and then you're in a bind.'

'Why wait until dark?'

Pine shot Kitty a look.

'What choice have we got?'

'Josh could walk back down the hill, now, and tell Silva someone's broken into Kitty Mac's saloon.'

Pine thought about that. 'Then horses are the problem. The livery barn's across the street from the jail.'

'When you've opened the cell, walk out the *front* door,' Notion said. 'Jax Silva'll be in here, dazzled by Kitty's charms.'

'And examining the broken lock,' Kitty said, and pointed to the back door.

Pine grinned. 'Didn't that happen when he was here?'

'Seconds before he arrived. Besides, so what? Either way, it's no lie.'

'There's one more problem,' Pine said slowly. 'Wilson's in the cell across from Gatlin. He's threatened to scream blue murder if we don't take him along.'

'Then do so,' Notion said. 'But only as far as the open door of his cell.' He looked at Pine, deadpan. 'You might have to use your er . . . ingenuity to stop him hollering. When that's done, make sure he's locked up again.'

And, once again, Pine felt his lips twitch in a grin.

12

Pine went first. He crossed over from the saloon and strolled down the far plank walk, his footsteps hard and hollow on the dry timber as he soaked up the sunshine with his Stetson tipped back. He was a Pinkerton operative who'd done his best, but had washed his hands of the whole affair now a risky client was back in jail. He was walking aimlessly, thinking about his next job.

And, yes, it was a working day. Businesses were open, shoppers and workers were walking up and down both sides of the street, and dust rose in clouds as people crossing the street weaved their way through wagons and horsemen clattering and rumbling over ruts that had already dried to a sun-baked hardness.

The hustle and bustle, Pine decided,

was a blessing. Before too long the town marshal would leave his office in the company of Josh Notion, and walk with him up to the saloon. A short while after that, two men were going to walk across the street from the jail and collect their horses from the livery stable.

Amid all the activity on Main Street they would go unnoticed then, and minutes later, when they rode out of town.

Pine reached the bottom of the street, glanced at the hotel in passing. The front door was closed. A quick look up at the second floor revealed a face at the window directly above room two. The man ducked back when he saw Pine watching.

And then the Pinkerton man was out of the sunlight and in the straw-smelling coolness of the livery stable. The hostler listened to Pine's instructions, spat a stream of tobacco juice and wandered away to saddle Pine's sorrel mare and Gatlin's roan. Pine wandered to the big double doors. He stood in the shadows to one side, and gazed up the hill.

After a few minutes wait he saw Josh Notion come around the bend by the stone bank building. He walked briskly down the hill, nodding and smiling at acquaintances, glanced once at the livery stable when he reached the flat then turned into the jail and shut the door.

Pine remained where he was. He heard the horses stepping lightly up the runway behind him, the gruff murmurings of the hostler.

Across the street the door to the jail was still shut. Pine tried to imagine what was happening in there. Would Silva fall for Notion's story? Or would he realize that the break-in Notion was talking about had been done by Green, only seconds before the marshal burst into the back room to arrest Jim Gatlin?

Pine smiled, appreciating Kitty Mac's deviousness and praying that it would work.

He watched idly as a black top-buggy came around the tall trees on the flat outskirts of town, pulled by a high-stepping pony. As the rig drew nearer he saw that the driver was the man called Green, and he felt the skin tighten across his cheekbones. A young woman sat at his side, clutching a briefcase. Her dark hair was lifted from her neck by the breeze as they trotted past. A rider was close behind them. Mundt. The unshaven gunman glanced towards the livery stable. Pine took half a step backwards.

Then the buggy was on its jolting way up the hill. Pine watched it pull in alongside the bank.

Across the street the jail door opened. Josh Notion came out, followed by Jax Silva. The marshal shut the door. The two men walked up the hill.

Charlie Pine let his breath go in a ragged exhalation.

He turned to the hostler. The old man had the two horses, their reins held tight in arthritic hands.

'Hold them there,' Pine said. 'I'll be a couple of minutes, no more.'

∗   ∗   ∗

Gatlin was dozing on the cot in his cell when he heard the murmur of voices in the office. He opened his eyes. It sounded like . . . Silva . . . and Josh Notion? He frowned. A strip of blue sky could be seen through the high barred window. Gatlin estimated that it was still some way short of midday. Listening to the murmured conversation, he swung his legs off the cot and sat up. Wilson was watching him from the other cell.

Notion said something. Jax Silva laughed. The outer door opened, then slammed shut. Silence. No movement. Not even the sound of the marshal moving about the office.

Gatlin looked at Wilson. The outlaw's eyes were wary. He shrugged.

Then the front door opened again.

Footsteps, treading carefully. A moment of silence, as if the newcomer was standing still, watching and listening. Then the sudden loud jingling of keys.

The inner door opened.

Charlie Pine came through from the office.

In one hand he was carrying the welded metal ring holding the keys to the cells. In the other he had Gatlin's six-gun.

'Hallelujah,' Wilson said softly.

'Change of plan,' Pine said quietly, and he put a finger to his lips as he looked at Gatlin.

'That old deputy's out there. Ned Riley. Fast asleep in Silva's chair. Whatever you do, keep your voice down.'

He was already trying keys in the cell door. He found the right one and carefully, silently opened the lock. The door swung on oiled hinges. Pine closed his eyes in relief. Gatlin stepped out into the passage.

Pine handed him his six-gun.

Across the passage, Wilson was up off the cot and clutching the bars. His eyes were narrowed as he watched Pine.

'I hope you two ain't forgot the deal,' he said in a cautious whisper.

'Deal?'

'That's the way I see it. I go with you, or nobody's goin' anywhere.'

Pine crossed to his cell. Wilson relaxed, grinned and stepped back. Pine again found the right key. He opened the door and eased it open. He half turned away from Wilson, caught Gatlin's eye, and winked.

Almost imperceptibly, Gatlin nodded. He backed a couple of paces up the passageway. Wilson stepped cautiously out of the cell, but he was being forced to look in two directions at the same time. Pine was in front of him, Gatlin behind. And Wilson's first glance was towards Pine.

Jaw tight, Gatlin took a pace forward. He swung the six-gun like a club and felled the outlaw with a single blow to

138

the skull, caught him as he slumped to the floor.

'Get him back inside.'

Gatlin nodded. Together they lifted the unconscious man's dead weight back into the cell and onto the cot. Gatlin turned him on his side, facing the wall, and covered him with the blanket.

'And now?'

Pine jerked a thumb. 'We walk out. Like a couple of ghosts.'

'Where's Silva?'

'Up at the saloon with Josh Notion, investigating last night's break-in.'

'Notion's idea?'

'Nope. Kitty Mac's.'

Gatlin smiled and shook his head in wonder. 'Let's go. That's not going to keep him there all day.'

They left without hurrying, tiptoeing through the office where the sleeping old deputy's moustache fluttered with his deep breathing, stepping out into the hot sunshine and standing non-chalantly on the plank walk for a few moments engaged in meaningless conversation while their eyes searched the street in both directions for signs of danger.

Then they walked across the street to the livery stable. Halfway there, Pine nudged Gatlin. With a covert, sidelong look he followed the direction of the other man's eyes and realized they were being watched from the hotel. Second floor, above his old room; and without being told he knew that the watcher was one of the other outlaws, River, or Hidalgo.

When they walked into the livery stables the roan pricked up its ears and whickered softly. Pine paid the hostler as Gatlin swung into the saddle, then followed suit and both men rode out into the street.

And now Pine was at a loss.

'Which way?'

'If your heart can stand the strain, I say we cut along the side of the jail and follow the alley that takes us all the way up to the rear of the saloon.'

'What the hell for?'

Gatlin grinned. 'The amazing Kitty Mac keeps rifles in the kitchen, and we're short on fire power.'

'What about Silva? He's still up there.'

'I've got a feeling Josh Notion will keep him in the bar.'

'Come on! The man's up there to investigate a break-in. He's *forced* to go into that back room to do his job.' Pine pulled the sorrel back. 'And now there's another problem. That old deputy's woke up. He's standing in the doorway, soaking up the sun.'

'Let him be. He doesn't know me; he doesn't know you. Keep going.'

The roan had already picked its way across the rutted street. With Pine close behind, Gatlin cut down the alley alongside the jail and turned into the longer alley that ran parallel to Main Street all the way to the top of the hill. The alley was littered with rubbish, the backs of the various buildings revealing the decay that on the elevations facing

Main Street was hidden by painted false fronts.

Harness jingled. The horses snorted and blew as they climbed the hill. When they reached the point where the alley swung to the left Gatlin knew they were passing the bank. Another block, one more side alley crossed, and they had reached the fence where he had tied the roan and he was once again looking at the back of the saloon.

The door, he noticed with some trepidation, was ajar.

Pine reined in behind him.

Gatlin swung down, and handed the reins to the Pinkerton man. He stepped up to the back door, and listened. The murmur of voices — but they appeared to be distant, the sounds coming through from the bar. Cautiously, Gatlin eased the back door fully open. The hinges creaked. He bit his lip, grimaced — then gingerly stepped inside.

Like a bright yellow flame, Kitty Mac was coming through the doorway leading to the bar.

She gasped, clapped a hand to moist red lips. Then she reached back and carefully closed the door behind her.

'What the hell are you doing here?' she whispered.

'Charlie Pine's outside with the horses. We're leaving, but I need a rifle,' Gatlin said.

'Take one.' Kitty's face was pink with fright. 'Take one and go, get out of here. You know Silva's been in here, looking at the door? You know he's *still* here, probably listening?'

'Of course I know,' Gatlin said. 'But when I met you and Josh, everything changed. From now on, nothing can go wrong.'

He crossed the room and took a Winchester from the rack, a box of shells from the shelf. Then he went to Kitty — still standing with her back to the closed door — and bent to plant a kiss on her forehead.

'I won't tell you where we're going,' he said, 'so that when Silva asks you

— and you can be damn sure he will
— you won't have to lie.' He touched
the tip of her nose lightly with his
finger, and winked. 'But we *will* be back
— and you can be damn sure of that,
too.'

Then he crossed the room and
slipped out through the broken back
door.

13

In the Cedar Creek hotel, Hidalgo was pacing the floor. His dark face was twisted with fury. Every now and then he'd stop his pacing at the window, flick aside the curtain and glance out.

River was lounging on one of the beds. He said, 'For Christ's sake sit down, you're making me nervous.'

'So where have they gone?' Hidalgo said, swinging around. 'What are they doing? What are *we* going to do about Wilson?'

'Wilson can wait,' River said. 'He's got a roof over his head, a bed, and free food. He can sit there all day admiring his plans, thinking about the money.'

'Plans? His plans are already in ruins because of those two, Gatlin and that Pinkerton *tipo*.'

'So we go after them, and put everything right.'

'Where? If we are to do that we should be following them *now*, but they are already long gone.'

'Yeah, but if you'd been usin' your puny Mex' brain you'd *know* where they've gone.'

Hidalgo came away from the window and flung himself down on the other bed. He found a thin cheroot in his pocket. A match flared.

'Yes,' he said, and suddenly he grinned through the cloud of blue smoke. 'That horse we saw — am I right?'

'Dead right. A blue roan, tethered up there in the woods when we rode in. Up against those cliffs, the glow of a fire.'

'And just now,' Hidalgo said, 'Gatlin rode out of town — on a blue roan.'

'We don't know he rode out of town, because he went into that alley by the jail. But where else would he be going?'

'After Hood's money?'

River shook his head. 'He's like us. He knows Hood's around here, some-where — but up to now that's all he

146

knows. People in this town are close-mouthed. *They* know where Hood is, but for their own good, they ain't saying.'

'All this is true,' Hidalgo said, frowning. 'But if so, how can going after Gatlin put things right?'

'Maybe it won't put everything right,' River said, 'but we can make damn sure after tonight Gatlin won't be poking his nose in where it ain't wanted — you understand me, *amigo*?'

'Ah, *sí*, I understand only too well,' Hidalgo said, and as he drew his revolver and twirled it on his forefinger the white teeth clamped on the thin cheroot flashed in a broad grin.

★ ★ ★

In the saloon, Marshal Jax Silva was at the bar tossing back a shot of whiskey alongside Josh Notion when Kitty Mac returned from the back room. He watched the dividing door open, the buxom blonde saloon-keeper walk through and meet his gaze with a challenging glance as she sashayed behind the bar. When she climbed onto her usual tall stool against the bottle shelves he noticed the pink blossoming on her cheeks, the rapid rise and fall of her ample breasts beneath the bodice of the yellow dress — and belatedly he put two and two together.

'I must be getting too old for this job,' he said.

'Comes to us all,' Notion said.

'That's not to take credit away. You worked it well — and like a fool I fell for it.'

Kitty sniffed. 'I don't know what you're talking about — but whatever it is, you're taking it well.'

Silva shrugged. 'That's because I couldn't hold him without charge. I started off on the wrong foot the minute he rode into town. Against my better judgement I listened to Lane Green, went along with his harebrained scheme. That's over. I'm bound by the law. So I knew, sooner or later,

I'd have to release him.'

'Release who?'

'The man you were talking to out there in the back room. Jim Gatlin. The man Charlie Pine just got out of jail.'

'How'd he manage that?' Notion said. 'I saw Ned Riley when I was down there, wasn't he supposed to be minding the store?'

'Ned Riley,' Silva said, 'was asleep before you and me stepped out into the street.'

Kitty smiled beneficently. 'But if a prisoner has escaped, and if we *were* involved — and I'm not saying we were — you know we did it to protect you, Jax. Like you said, you *were* acting illegally.'

'Yeah, thanks a million; now go tell that to Hood.'

'You think Gatlin's a threat to the big man?'

'I think he's a threat — one of several that's rode into town — and thanks to you, he's on the loose.'

'If I were you,' Josh Notion said, 'I'd

concentrate on those other Texas hardcases over at the hotel.'

'There's a point,' Silva said, eyes narrowing. 'I had one of 'em locked up in the cell across from Gatlin. Do you suppose Wilson walked out when Pine opened the doors?'

Notion's eyebrows lifted in pained innocence. 'Now, Jax, how the hell would we know?'

★ ★ ★

'All right,' Belinda Hood said, 'then what do you recommend?'

When she was inside the bank taking the bundles of notes being passed across the counter to her and stowing them in the briefcase, she had been aware of the odd glances, the swiftly averted eyes; the sense that something was terribly wrong.

She had mentioned it to Lane Green when she climbed up to sit alongside him on the top-buggy. He had shrugged, and looked away as he flicked the reins

150

— another odd reaction.

Silva's white Stetson had been visible some way ahead of them as he hurried down the hill. When the top-buggy pulled in and Belinda walked into the jail, he was emerging from the cell block. There was palpable relief on his face. He had listened to her general concern, then brought her up to date on developments — and it had been clear to Belinda that he was inwardly seething.

Now, having heard the latest news, she was standing in front of the desk putting a direct question to the somewhat shamefaced town marshal who was swinging nervously back and forth in his swivel chair.

Silva frowned. 'I recommend you do nothing.'

'That's absurd. You couldn't hold Jim Gatlin. How sure can I be that you'll keep that other man locked up?'

'At the moment he's nursing a sore head. Gatlin or Pine knocked him unconscious. His cronies are over the street in the hotel. My guess is they won't move without Wilson. And, believe me, he's going nowhere.'

'If one man can snatch a prisoner from under the nose of a deputy, two men can do the same.'

'Once bitten . . . ' Silva shook his head. 'No, that ain't going to happen.'

'But if it does?'

'Jesus Christ, Belinda, will you give over!' Silva stopped swinging and leaned forward to slam both hands down on the desk. 'If it does, then you've got Jim Gatlin and three Texas hardcases out there and every damn one of 'em after your pa's cash. You knew it would happen; you *knew* it was only a matter of time — but if and when it comes to that, I'll be ready.'

Belinda touched her loose dark hair, a small frown creasing her smooth brow.

'I'm going home now, and there will be questions asked. What do I tell him?'

'Nothing. There's no need to raise the alarm.'

'There is — because despite what you say, I cannot believe you. All right, you say you *will* be ready. But Cedar Creek has always been a small town unused to trouble of any kind. You are just one man with good intentions relying on an ageing deputy who uses all his energy trying to stay awake. To be convinced you mean business I'd need to see all four men behind bars, and at least two young deputies making sure those four get to trial — '

'They've done nothing.'

'What do you mean?'

'You know exactly what I mean. To slam a man in the hoosegow I've got to believe or suspect he's committed a crime. Gatlin robbed the Atchison Topeka many years ago, and paid the penalty. The others — well, as far as I know they've committed no crime, no reward notices have come through . . . '

'Your point being?'

'I was holding Gatlin without charge. Now I've got Wilson — but I don't know how long I can hold him locked up.' Silva sighed. 'Years ago, I told your pa I'd do my best to protect him, his family, his money. This is the first time there's been a threat, but until one or all of these men make a move, there's nothing I can do.'

★ ★ ★

For a few minutes after Belinda Hood had walked out, Marshal Jax Silva sat at his desk, one finger idly playing with the typewriter keys, his mind busy.

Abruptly, he stood up and went through to the cell block.

Secure behind strap-steel bars, Wilson was lying on his cot in exactly the same position as he had been when Silva walked in and found him. Then, the Texan had been unconscious; now he was asleep, no doubt retreating into darkness away from the pain of a bursting headache.

Well, he could stay where he was — at least until he woke up.

Silva looked across at the open door

of the other cell, and smiled ruefully at the ease with which Jim Gatlin had been snatched from custody. It showed weaknesses in the system, Silva thought — if anything in Cedar Creek could be said to work to a system.

A long time ago, one man had replaced a small town's democracy with a dictatorship founded on money apparently honestly acquired. Was that grip now, finally, being loosened by outsiders who were themselves lawless? Had the truth come from the mouths of those more accustomed to lying? And if it had, Jax Silva wondered, was it now time for him to decide once and for all whose side he was on?

Maybe.

The question was still tormenting him when he returned to the office. Instead of trying to find an answer, Silva poked at the stove, got the coffee brewing and sat down to ruminate on a situation that was going from bad to worse.

He was sure of one thing: every crisis

he had ever faced at some point ran out of time. When it did, it was resolved — one way or another. And that, he knew, was the problem. Like all others, the crisis facing the Hoods would be resolved.

Trouble was, with different outlaw factions lured from Texas by a powerful man's fortune that was mostly kept as cash in a private residence tucked away in the hills, the only way anyone could come out top dog was by resorting to bloodshed, and death.

Sorting that lot out, Silva mused, was a lot to ask of an old deputy liable to fall asleep in the sun, and a small-town marshal fighting an inner battle with issues of loyalty linked to self-preservation.

Was it time to use hard rocks to blunt a sharp knife? Was it high time he quit fooling about, and used his cunning to recruit a couple of gullible deputies?

14

Dinner for Jim Gatlin and Charlie Pine was fried pork and beans cooked to a greasy sizzling, flavoured by the wood fire and washed down with coffee as they hunkered at the mouth of the cave that was Gatlin's base camp. As they ate they listened idly to the sounds of the roan and sorrel grazing on a patch of grass higher up the slope between cliff face and trees, more intently to the whisper of birds and small animals and the clicking of the woods as the day's heat faded.

If they had been followed — or if River and Hidalgo had watched from the hotel as they left town but were waiting for dark to make their move — it would be those latter sounds that would abruptly cease. There could be no clearer warning than the sudden, awful silence that would follow.

And both Gatlin and Pine knew that the outlaws' coming was as inevitable as the approaching dusk.

It was late afternoon. They had taken their dinner early, going by the maxim that in dangerous times a man eats when he can, or risks going hungry. Now both men had spread their blankets close to the entrance, placed saddles at the head of the makeshift beds for pillows, and were lying back discussing tactics.

'What beats me,' Gatlin said, 'is I've been in or around Cedar Creek almost two days and everything's been so damn crazy I've had no time to ask directions to Hood's spread. So, if we get through tonight — that's what I do next.'

'Waste of time even if you do get around to it,' Pine said. 'I've been here much longer. Talk about Hood to anyone in town and they clam up.'

Gatlin frowned. 'Why? He's been in this area for years.'

'And everyone knows where he lives?

Sure. Of course they do. But when a man controls a town, would you risk being the one to give away his location to an ex-con who's ridden a thousand miles to kill him?'

Gatlin thought for a moment.

'I know of two people who'd be willing to give us directions.'

Pine chuckled. 'They'd do more than that. I've got a feeling Josh Notion would be pleased to ride with you and confront Hood.'

'So — no problem?'

'Well . . . ' Pine frowned. 'Think about what we left when we rode out. Wilson was unconscious in a cell. Notion had lured Silva away from the jail so I could get you out. You sneaked a rifle off Kitty Mac in the back room — almost out from under Silva's nose, because he was standing in the bar.'

'Put that way,' Gatlin said, 'he's got good reason to throw the both of them in jail.'

'On the other hand,' Pine said, 'I have serious doubts about Jax Silva's commitment to Nathan Hood. I think the man's powerful hold is weakening.'

'You sowed the seeds of doubt.' Gatlin nodded when Pine looked surprised. 'When I told Silva my story he'd already listened to your version of events. What you overheard in the hotel has shaken his belief in Nathan Hood.'

'It was happening anyway. When a man becomes a recluse, enemies take it as a sign of fading power.'

'That's good for me if I'm — '

Gatlin stopped abruptly and jerked his head up as something hit the hanging coffee pot a mighty blow. The metal rang like a cracked bell. Hot coffee sprayed over the two men and sent a cloud of steam hissing from the fire and into the cave. In that same instant Gatlin and Pine rolled frantically out of their blankets as the crack of the shot split the air.

★　★　★

A deafening volley of shots followed that first shocking crack of a rifle. Hot lead screamed into the cave. Bullets sent sparks showering from the stone walls. Ricochets howled like animals keening. Muzzle flashes danced madly on the cave's roof like flames reflected from angry waters.

Gatlin cursed his stupidity.

A safe refuge was turning into a death trap, leaving them with terrible decisions to make. They could choose the manner of their dying: burst from the mouth of the cave with six-guns blazing, or retreat into the darkness of a stone tunnel where hot lead hissed and whined from the walls and from which there could be no escape.

The third option was surrender — but with at least two rifles pouring a hail of lead into the cave the best they could do at that moment was to scrape a hole in the rock floor with their fingernails while lying flat enough to stay alive.

The volley ceased. Silence was almost

painful. Gatlin and Pine, face down on the gritty rock with their hands locked behind their heads, opened their eyes cautiously.

Gatlin squinted at Pine.

'They out of ammunition?'

'Wore their trigger fingers out,' Pine said, and grinned.

Then a voice rang out from the woods.

'This is the law. You're trapped. Throw down your weapons and come out of the cave.'

Gatlin frowned. 'That's not Silva.'

'No.'

'And it doesn't sound like a creaking old deputy out for target practice.'

'What it sounds like,' Pine said, 'is a man called River.'

Gatlin's eyes widened. 'If that's River and there's just the two of them, then the other man's Hidalgo and somebody's lying through their teeth.'

'Maybe not.'

Gatlin cursed softly. 'You saying Silva swore them in and gave them a couple of tin badges?'

'If I am,' Pine said, 'then I was wrong about his faltering allegiance.'

'Or maybe we just underestimated his ingenuity.'

'Yeah. He's resorted to dirty tricks, playing one against — '

Another shout.

'You two in there — you hear me?'

'I hear you,' Gatlin called.

'This here's Deputies River and Hidalgo out of the Cedar Creek marshal's office. Our orders are to bring you in. Come on out, now, with your hands up.'

'Go to hell,' Pine roared. 'It's a stand-off. We can't come out; you're stuck out there in the woods — and it's getting dark.'

The answer was another withering volley of rifle fire. Again Gatlin and Pine hugged the stone floor. Rock chippings rained down, hot needles stinging exposed skin. Bullets kicked up the fire's embers. Dust and smoke were sucked into the cave.

Coughing, watching what was happening through eyes that stung and watered, Gatlin blocked his mind to the rattle of gunfire and did some thinking. The first time he'd visited the cave, he'd lit a fire. Late that day he'd rebuilt his fire, and watched the smoke drift *into the cave*. A few minutes ago, the first bullet had knocked the coffee pot loose and smoke and steam had drifted *into the cave*. Now another bullet had scattered the fire, and the dust and smoke were going into the cave — *as if being sucked in that direction*.

Gatlin rolled onto his back as the gunfire ceased. Waited. Pine said something. Gatlin waved him into silence. Then came the expected hail from the woods.

'You ready to come out while you're still alive?'

'Maybe,' Gatlin said. 'Give us time to think this through.'

'No. You come out, or we come and get you.'

Gatlin laughed. 'You're talking bull. Like my friend told you, it's a stand-off. So far we've not fired a shot. But you come running out of the trees and up the slope and you'll be picking six-gun slugs out of your teeth.'

Silence. Gatlin looked at Pine. The Pinkerton man opened his mouth to speak. Again Gatlin wagged a silencing finger.

Then he got his answer from the woods.

'All right. You've got five minutes, no more. After that — '

'After that you'd better hope I've come up with something,' Gatlin answered, 'or we'll all be here till Christmas.'

And then he scrambled to his feet.

'Come on, Charlie, grab your saddle and let's get out of here.'

'You *what*!'

'We're going out the back door. There's another opening. Has to be, the way that smoke's been getting sucked into the cave.'

The operative caught on fast.

'You clever son of a gun,' he muttered, and sprang to his feet.

'He's given us five minutes,' Gatlin said, 'but we can stretch that any way we like because the only way they'll risk attacking this little stronghold is under cover of darkness.'

And darkness of the most fearful kind, Gatlin thought, is what we're about to face.

Outside dusk was rapidly approaching. Ten paces in from the mouth of the cave and they were struggling to see. Another ten paces — which took them down a dip and around the first bend in a narrowing passage — and they were feeling their way like men struck blind.

Gatlin slung the saddle over his shoulder, stretched out his right arm and slid his hand along the rough wall as he took one cautious pace, then another. He could hear Pine behind him, his harsh breathing, the scrape of his clothes as he too brushed along the stone wall. Proceeding in that manner they stumbled over the uneven floor of the cave, slipped on loose rocks, banged painfully against unseen projections.

Cobwebs touched their skin like ghostly fingers. Something rustled overhead, and Gatlin visualized bats hanging upside down — and shivered.

Then, as the air turned dank, he heard running water. Seconds later his feet splashed into an icy pool.

'Jesus,' he whispered — and Charlie Pine bumped into his back.

'The air's cold and strong on the back of my neck,' Pine said. 'I just hope the hole up ahead's big enough for a man to crawl through.'

Gatlin said nothing. He took a step forward, then another, and it was like walking downstairs in the dark. Then he was in up to his knees, cold water pouring into his boots.

'How'd you like swimming in the dark, Charlie?'

'Hell, I can't swim in *daylight*.'

'Here. Hold my saddle.'

'Two saddles — with a broken hand?'

'Rest yours.'

Gatlin dug around in his pockets, found a lucifer, snapped it into life with his thumbnail. The match flared. The flame bent in the draught. Gatlin cupped the match in his hands, nursed the flame; opened his hand and let the weak light shine ahead.

And let his pent breath go in a gasp of relief.

The water was trickling down one damp wall and across the floor of the cave to gurgle away into a shiny black fissure in the rock. Over centuries the constant flow had worn a wide gully across the stone floor. Gatlin was standing in the middle of it. Ahead, the rocky floor was bone dry and dusty as far as yet another bend.

Beyond that there was the unknown.

Gatlin let the match hiss into the water. He splashed out onto the dry floor, spent precious seconds emptying the water from his boots then fumbled his saddle from Pine. Imprinted on his mind was what he had seen by the light of the match. He strode forward confidently until he judged he was nearing the bend. Again he reached out for the wall, followed it with his hand. Then the stone surface curved away from him.

He'd reached the bend. He worked his way around it. Stopped. Squeezed his eyes tight shut, then opened them.

He'd not been mistaken. Ahead, and high up to his left, there was a sliver of light.

'I'm with you,' Pine said hoarsely at his shoulder. 'And if that's the opening it looks awful small.'

'I asked if you could swim in the dark,' Gatlin said. 'Maybe I should have asked if you can fly.'

'Strike a match. If there's no other way up I'll start flapping my arms.'

Gatlin grinned in the dark, then acknowledged the pointless gesture with a shake of the head.

'Let's get closer first,' he said.

Again, cautiously, they felt their way forward. The overhead gap seemed to widen, the light became brighter; it was dusk outside, but compared with the stygian darkness of the cave the patch

169

of sky looked as bright as a summer's day.

Then Gatlin stumbled, and went down. He clenched his teeth as sharp rocks bit into his knees. With his hands, he explored the barrier that had brought him down.

'Pile of rubble,' he said — and something in his voice imbued those three words with enormous, magical potential.

Swiftly he fumbled for his matches, found one, scraped it into life.

'A stairway to the stars,' Pine said reverently, and his chuckle was an outpouring of relief.

They had moved into a vast chamber. Light from the flame faded before it could reach the surrounding walls. Immediately in front of them a tumbled heap of fallen rocks lead steeply up to the fissure. At some time in the past a fault in the rock vault must have given way. Gradually the weather had enlarged the crack. Ice and snow had crumbled the rock, sent each piece tumbling into the cave to crash onto the growing pile.

'Ten thousand years,' Gatlin said softly, 'just settin' there waiting for you and me.'

'Be a shame to let it wait any longer,' Pine said, and he brushed past Gatlin.

It was more a scramble than a climb. Pine went first. Handicapped by his broken hand he slipped once, and Gatlin broke his fall by holding him with shoulder and braced legs. Steady again, Pine looked back and grinned, his face pale in the light leaking through the crack. Then he turned back to the climb and within seconds they had reached the top.

Close up, the fissure was a horizontal slit in the rock. It looked too narrow — but Pine pushed his saddle through then hooked a leg and an arm into the gap and squirmed through face down.

Gatlin followed.

They were on a grassy ledge. The woods were spread out beneath them like a carpet of dark green. They could see the lights of Cedar Creek to the south-west, and even at that height the bite of spent gunpowder was carried to their nostrils on the cool night air.

'What about the horses?' Pine said. 'All that shooting . . . '

'If I know you, Pinkerton man, you've trained that sorrel to stand stock still in a thunderstorm — just like I've trained my roan. They'll be there.'

'Maybe — but as I crawled out I thought I heard hoofs.'

'If you heard hoofs — and I hope you did — that would be Silva's new deputies heading for home.'

'Only one way to find out. We've climbed up, now we climb down.'

In the gathering gloom they trudged uphill then worked their way to their right and slithered down a long, easy slope that brought them to the strip of open ground at the foot of the cliffs. The horses, Gatlin knew, were tethered on a grassy patch somewhere below them. Beyond the horses, in the woods, River and Hidalgo could be holed up, waiting.

'Hear anything more?'

Pine shook his head.

'So we move down nice and slow. If our horses are still there — and you *did* hear riders — River and Hidalgo are long gone.'

It was almost full dark. Gatlin led the way. Fifty yards down the slope he could smell the smouldering embers of the camp-fire. Another ten and he stumbled and sent a stone rattling down the slope and into the trees. He held his breath. Then he heard a soft whicker ahead of him. Moments later they'd reached the horses.

Gatlin put down the saddle and stepped up close to the roan. He cupped its warm muzzle in his hand, fondled its ears and whispered soothing words, all the while listening and watching Pine as he too dropped his saddle then slipped like a shadow into the woods.

He was back within minutes.

'Gone. I found their position. Couldn't

miss it. Shells everywhere, shining like glow worms in the dark.' Then he grinned. 'Here.'

He tossed two bundles onto the ground, and Gatlin realized the Pinkerton man had been into the cave and retrieved their bedrolls.

'If River and Hidalgo have left,' he said, 'there's nothing stopping us sleeping in the cave.'

'Nothing stopping you,' Pine said. 'I wouldn't go back in that black hole for a half share in Hood's massive fortune — besides, those two *hombres* could return. So, get your head down, my friend. I always did rely on hunches, and something's telling me that by tomorrow night you'll be rich, or dead.'

The way it was to turn out, Gatlin would be neither — but, as he followed Pine into the woods and unrolled his blankets on the carpet of dry leaves, his thoughts were with a small-town marshal who had cajoled help from a wily Pinkerton op then played both ends against the middle by deputizing two known outlaws.

The lawman was playing a devious game. Why? — and what the hell would he do next?

15

The question lingered with Gatlin throughout an almost sleepless night. Not coming up with an answer, knowing that Silva's next move could profoundly affect his own plans, he woke Pine well before dawn and in the chill of that unearthly hour they saddled up and set off on the short ride to Cedar Creek.

'What plans?' Pine grumbled once, and for the duration of the ride Gatlin again was forced to leave a question unanswered.

When the lights of the town appeared, turned wan by the brighter light flaming in the east, he called a halt.

'This is getting to be a habit,' he said. 'I stopped under these trees two nights ago and watched you ride up to the saloon in the rain; saw Jax Silva doing his rounds.'

'Why stop now?' Pine said — then shook his head. 'Stupid question. Two men on horseback ride into Cedar Creek at dawn. Silva and his new deputies spot them — guess who?'

'I'll pose a different question. You're right, I have no plan — so what do we do next?'

'You already answered that one.'

'What — talk to Kitty Mac and Notion?'

'Who else do you know will take kindly to a dawn visit?'

Gatlin looked across at Main Street. 'Notion's gun shop's too far down the hill.'

'Yes, and I've still got a room in the hotel — but that's also directly across the street from Silva's office.'

'So it's Kitty's place.'

'And with that settled, there's just the horses to consider. Tying them out front would be announcing our presence.'

Gatlin thought for a moment.

'There's a gully behind those buildings. It cuts south through the trees. We put the horses in there they won't be seen . . . '

They rode across the head of a deserted Main Street, skirted the ramshackle empty building and crossed the alley. Moments later, the horses tethered out of sight, they approached the back of the saloon. It was in darkness. Gatlin led the way.

'Do I detect a man in a hurry?'

'Come on, Charlie! I'm chasing the man who ruined my life. It took us most of a year to find him. Wilson and his cronies managed that in less than a month . . . '

The back door's latch was still broken. Gatlin remembered the wedge holding it shut. Pushing it would not get him inside, but there was one thing it would do.

'If Kitty's bedroom window over-looks Main Street,' Pine said, 'we're in trouble.'

'I don't know where she sleeps, but I do know she's got sharp ears.'

Gatlin stepped back, lifted his leg

parallel to the ground and hit the door a mighty blow with the sole of his right boot. It sounded as if a charge of dynamite had been detonated in the back room. The door bowed inwards at the top, then snapped back with a sound like a pistol shot. The bottom, held firm by the wedge, didn't move.

Gatlin hit the door again. Then again. The thunderous explosions echoing through the building must have sounded like an artillery assault. Again Gatlin lifted his foot. He launched yet another piston-like kick, and felt the massive shock jar his knee and hip.

The door rocked again, and something came loose. On the other side, the wedge screeched across the floor. A gap opened. In the gap a face more angry than apprehensive glared at them from under tousled blonde hair. Lower down, a shotgun held in nervous hands threatened to blow them both to pieces. Kitty Mac's red lips tightened. Then she stepped back. Gatlin heard her kick the wedge, swear softly as she hurt her toes. The door creaked open.

Kitty Mac went to the lamp and turned up the wick as Gatlin and Pine walked in and pushed the door to. She looked at Gatlin's face.

'You heal fast.'

'Bruises do, not broken bones. Charlie's hand will take longer.'

The saloon-keeper stifled a yawn that was part tiredness, part shock. And now there was impatience in her blue eyes as she banged the coffee pot on the iron stove where logs hissed and crackled.

'So, why the hell have I been dragged out of bed?'

'Last night we were dodging bullets fired at us by Silva's two new deputies.'

'Two new ones?' Kitty paused, frowning.

'That's right. River and Hidalgo.'

Kitty had one hand on the coffee pot, the other on her padded hip. Her eyes had gone from impatience to disbelief.

'Are you telling me Jax slams one night rider in the cooler and pins badges on the other two?'

'Charlie thinks it's a cunning plan,' Gatlin said, and sat down at the table. 'Silva's playing both ends against the middle. He was hoping for a bloody shoot out well away from town, everyone winding up dead.'

'I can see two still standing so that didn't work well for him. What about the others, are they dead?'

'No. It's a long story. Cut short, we think they rode back to town after dark.'

'They'd have gone back to the hotel for the night. But this morning they'll be talking to Jax.'

Charlie Pine grinned. 'When that happens your marshal will be holding a tiger by the tail and wondering how he can let go without getting mauled.'

'When he does let go,' Kitty said drily, 'he'll lose another prisoner.'

'But not before they get the location of Hood's place,' Gatlin said. 'You see, Charlie's got another theory: he thinks Jax Silva may be weary of being Hood's puppet lawman — but unsure which way to turn. Does he swallow his pride and stay loyal? — or sell Hood down the river? Either way, he's likely to be confused and let slip information he wouldn't normally divulge. And when Wilson's got that location, those owl-hoots will go after Hood.'

'Pardon me for being a heartless old biddy,' Kitty said, 'but why don't we let them do that?'

'Well, there is one small problem,' Gatlin said.

'No,' Pine said. 'There's no problem. Sure, there's a conflict of interest because you're also after Hood, but it's in your best interests to tackle those owlhoots. Get rid of them, you'll have a clear run.'

Gatlin pulled a face. 'You suggesting we launch an attack on the Cedar Creek marshal's office — in broad daylight?'

'I'm not sure what I'm suggesting — in fact I'm open to suggestions from the floor,' Pine said, and looked expectantly at Kitty.

She shook her head. 'Maybe I'm as confused as Jax. I'm all for stopping those owlhoots. And I know it's high time the town got rid of Hood. But I'm still not sure of your intentions, Jim Gatlin. Confronting the man who framed you is one thing, but . . . ' She hesitated. 'Haydn Crawford will have his ideas . . . and the town council . . . I don't know, maybe you should go talk to Josh.' Then she shook her head again. 'No, of course, you can't do that.' She hesitated. 'But maybe you can't wait too long, either?'

'If I was in their shoes,' Gatlin said, 'I'd make my move before the town wakes up.'

He watched Kitty Mac cross to the stove and pour coffee. When she passed the steaming cups around they sat at the table sipping the hot, black java for a while, each alone with their thoughts as they mulled over what had been said.

Eventually Gatlin caught Kitty Mac watching him. There was amusement in her blue eyes, along with a clear message. He shook his head as understanding dawned, then looked at Pine and grinned ruefully. It was the Pinkerton man who broke the silence.

'If they're one step ahead of you and about to make a move before the town wakes up, maybe we should get the jump on them by making a move before they make a move.'

'Yeah,' Gatlin said, 'I just worked that one out.'

But even as he uttered the words he knew he was too late. Almost like the gentle crackling and spitting coming from the black stove on the other side of the kitchen, he heard the distant crack of a single shot, then the sudden rattle as several six-guns opened fire.

16

Gunfire was still cracking intermittently when Gatlin and Pine tumbled out of the saloon's back door. They ran to their horses, raced up out of the gully and swung into Main Street. When they passed the front of the saloon Kitty was already there, poking her blonde head out of the front door and knotting the belt of her robe. At the corner by the bank Gatlin was several yards ahead of the one-handed Pinkerton man. He was vaguely aware of more doors opening. People were stepping onto the plank-walk yelling questions, then rushing into the street to look down the hill.

Then Gatlin's eyes caught the white puff of gunsmoke. One of the gunmen was firing across the street at the jail from the open doors of the livery stable.

Gatlin slowed the roan and glanced back. Pine had caught up with him. He too had spotted the tell-tale gunsmoke.

'Cut through to the alley.'

He was pointing right. Gatlin nodded. Pine was already following his own advice. He'd taken the sorrel across the street and was galloping into the gap between the buildings.

Gatlin knew the alley behind the premises on the north side of town would also run parallel to Main Street. If they followed it all the way down the hill they would reach the back of the hotel. Then what?

There was no time to think. Pine was riding like a madman. Gatlin followed recklessly. Tin cans rattled and danced under racing hoofs. Loose rocks popped into the undergrowth on his right. The roan was snorting with excitement.

Ahead of him Pine skidded the sorrel to a halt and vaulted from the saddle. Gatlin pulled the roan in against timber walls in a cloud of dust and swung down. The hotel towered above them. They were between the building and its backdrop of steeply wooded slopes. The next building was the café, then Josh Notion's premises — then the livery stable.

'Back door's open,' Gatlin said, and pulled his six-gun as he ran.

Pine was with him as they slipped in through the door. The wide runway sloped up to the street where sunlight flooded through open double doors. The smell of gunpowder was sharp in the air. In the stalls horses moved nervously. There was no sign of the hostler; no sign of any gunmen. And the shooting had ceased.

'Gone,' Pine said.

'If he's gone, he's across the street — and that's not good.'

Gatlin led the way cautiously up the runway. His eyes searched for movement, but there was nowhere for a man to hide. He reached the double doors. Hugging the shadows, he looked across the street at the jail.

'Door's been kicked open,' Pine said.

Gatlin could see raw white wood where the lock had torn away. There was no sign of life. He stepped cautiously into the street. A voice hailed him. When he looked left, Josh Notion was down on one knee outside his gun shop. He had a '73 Winchester trained on the jail.

'Where's the Pinkerton man?'

'Here,' Pine said, and showed his face.

'There's two men in there with Silva,' Notion said.

'That'll be River and Hidalgo,' Gatlin said, but Notion shook his head.

'Can't say for sure. They moved too fast. Their faces are covered.'

'Whoever it is,' Pine said, 'they'll get Wilson out if we don't do something.'

Notion grinned. 'I'll give you covering fire with this beauty. You youngsters are going to charge in there.'

Gatlin took a deep breath. He looked across the street. Fifty yards up from the jail, among other onlookers, he could see a tall, grey-haired man in a dark suit. He had walked down the hill from the bank, then stopped. Now he was watching them.

'Haydn Crawford,' Pine said. 'Head of the council.'

'All right, let's put on a show,' Notion said — and he opened up with the Winchester.

Gatlin went across the street in a swerving run. Pine did the same, ten yards to his left. Notion aimed a rapid fire between the two running men, raking the front of the jail. Bullets thudded into the stone walls, howled off the roof. The window shattered. Glass fell tinkling and glittering in the sunlight.

Gatlin leaped up onto the plankwalk. The Winchester fell silent. Pine joined Gatlin. They paused, either side of the open door, listening.

A heavy silence. Their eyes met. Then Pine shrugged — and sprang in through the doorway with his six-gun at the ready.

When Gatlin followed, Pine was already down on his knees alongside Jax Silva. The elegant marshal was flat on his back on the floor. His badge of

189

office and the front of his shirt were wet with blood. The once shrewd grey eyes were wide open and sightless.

There was no sign of the two men who had stormed the jail.

* * *

Half an hour later, the body of Marshal Jax Silva had been taken away. Four men were in his office. Haydn Crawford had assumed command and was sitting behind the desk. Josh Notion had one elbow on the window sill and from time to time glanced out through the shattered glass. Charlie Pine was sitting on the step in the open doorway leading to the cells. Gatlin had dragged the seat from in front of the desk and was sitting by the wall.

'The prisoner's still locked up because Silva hid the keys inside his shirt,' Crawford said. 'The men who killed him were either in too much of a hurry — thanks to Josh Notion pouring lead into the building — or they didn't want blood on their hands.' His tone was wry. 'But who were they? Did anybody see them?'

'Not clear enough to recognize,' Notion said. 'But we know the two men who'd want Wilson out of jail.'

'There's a problem there,' Charlie Pine said. 'Some time yesterday, Jax Silva deputized River and Hidalgo.'

'He what!' Haydn Crawford was astonished.

Gatlin was searching his memory. He said, 'We're going on their say so. Might have been a ruse to pry us out of that cave.' He was looking at Pine. The Pinkerton op spread his hands.

'Deputies or not,' Josh Notion said from the window, 'those two men have just left the hotel. They appear to be going next door for their breakfast.'

'Forget them, for now,' Haydn Crawford said. 'With no proof of wrongdoing, we'd be laughed out of court.' His brow was furrowed in thought. He dug a fat cigar out of his pocket, peeled off the wrapper, snipped off the end with a folding knife he found on Silva's desk. Then he scraped a match on the sole of his shoe and fired up the cigar.

'The last two days have been eventful, but the only big change is the town's without a marshal. His place has to be filled.' He looked around the room. 'Pine?'

Charlie Pine shook his head. 'I work for the Pinkertons. Charlie Eames would have a fit.'

'All right, what about you, Josh?'

'You serious? What about the deputy, Ned Riley?'

Crawford blew a cloud of smoke into the air and shook his head. 'Riley'll be asleep till noon then too bemused to think straight. And, since you ask, yes, I've never been more serious in my life. All right, you have a business to run so the position will be a stop-gap, but I can't think of anyone more suited for the job.'

★ ★ ★

After the swearing in of Josh Notion as town marshal, Gatlin and Pine retired to the Pinkerton op's hotel room and slept until noon. They ate a belated breakfast shortly after that in Millie's café, then strolled up the hill to the saloon. Kitty Mac eyed Gatlin with amusement as she set up drinks on the bar.

'I thought Marshal Notion would have driven you out of town.'

'Crawford's his boss, and he's more confused than Silva was. He can't find anything to pin on River and Hidalgo, Josh convinced him I'm harmless — '

'Hah! Josh is like me. He's not sure of your intentions.'

'I asked him to direct me to Hood's place. He refused.'

'I can just see you turning up there. You still look as if you walked into a tree with your face. If you didn't shoot him dead, Hood would die of fright.'

'We could ask around town,' Charlie Pine said, watching Kitty.

She shook her head. 'You could. And

you know the answer you'd get.'

Kitty wandered to the end of the bar to serve a new arrival. Gatlin led the way to a table near the window.

'Two days,' he said, fiddling with his drink. 'Two days — and where are we?'

'A year and two days,' Pine corrected.

'Right, and we're in the town that refuses to talk.'

'That's because it's a frightened town.'

'Maybe. That, or scared of losing even the precarious kind of security Hood's money brings. But what I saw in Kitty's eyes the first time I spoke to her and Josh was hope. Hope for others. People who have lost everything to Hood.'

'Sure, you're the knight on a big white horse. But you've got a rusty sword and your pennant's tattered — in a word, you're mistrusted.'

'They prefer what they've got to what I might bring — is that what you mean?'

194

'I don't know what I mean,' Charlie Pine said. 'But something's got to break soon or we'll all be too old.'

★ ★ ★

By evening Gatlin still had no idea what he was going to do about Hood.

Kitty had spent the afternoon sleeping, reappearing as Josh Notion walked into the saloon. Leaving a relief bartender in charge, they had gone through to the kitchen.

As darkness fell, Pine had gone down to the railroad to wire his Denver office; he'd decided to leave Cedar Creek the next day, Sunday.

Kitty and Notion were still in the back room when the saloon doors slapped open and Green and Mundt walked in. They saw Gatlin, flashed him a grin, then went to the bar.

A few minutes later Kitty and Josh reappeared. Kitty went behind the bar. Josh came over to the table where Gatlin had spent most of the day.

'I've got an idea,' Gatlin said.

'You're full of ideas,' Notion said. 'I've yet to hear a good one.'

'Green and Mundt are at the bar.'

'It's Saturday. It's their night to howl.'

'So they'll be here until late. If my arrival at the Hood place was going to cause trouble, it would come from those two. They're here in town, so now's a good time to confront the big man.'

'No.'

'Two of us. You and me. You there to keep the peace.'

Gatlin knew it was a way out of the deadlock; he could see he had Notion wobbling. As marshal, Notion had the responsibility to authorize the visit and the power to arrest Gatlin if it all went wrong. It was an offer he couldn't refuse.

'If you'd feel safer,' Gatlin said, 'I'll hand my weapons over to you and go in unarmed.'

Notion shook his head. 'No need for

196

that.' He got up from the table. 'I'll tell Kitty what's happening. You get your horse, I'll meet you down at the stables. You're about to get acquainted with the man you say sent you to the pen.'

17

Charlie Pine had wired details of his plans to Denver and was back in the saloon talking to Kitty when River and Hidalgo walked in. They ordered drinks from the relief man, then carried them along to the end of the bar where Green and Mundt were standing. After a few words Pine didn't catch, they retired to a table.

The four went into a huddle, their heads close together as they leaned on the table nursing their drinks. River seemed to be doing most of the talking. At first, Hood's men seemed uninterested in whatever was being said. Then, gradually, River began to talk them round and suddenly the 'breed, Hidalgo, was all flashing teeth.

But what were they being offered?

'I spoke to Belinda Hood a long time ago,' Kitty said, absently buffing a glass to a brilliant shine as she sat on her stool and watched the four men. 'She didn't say it right out, but I got the impression she didn't trust Green or Mundt.'

'Men like that will go where the money is,' Pine said. 'Hood's been good to them, but if there's a better offer — '

'They'll switch sides.' Kitty nodded. 'Instead of getting paid once a month they'll take a lump sum, thank you very kindly.'

'I wondered about that,' Charlie Pine said. 'There's all this talk of money, and Belinda's visits to the bank, but surely one medium-sized safe isn't going to be big enough to hold Hood's fortune.'

'Not if it was entirely in bank notes. But there'll be bonds, investments, policies, some cash — whatever's in there will be disposable.'

'So what's being discussed over there must be a four-way split — thieves doing a deal that'll never be honoured.'

'Doesn't matter,' Kitty said. 'River and Hidalgo need someone to take them to Hood. Who better than two restless gunslingers who've been working for Hood for too long on not much more than forty and found? Those Texans won't even have to ask. Give Green and Mundt a big enough carrot to sniff and they'll be *offering* to lead the way.'

'This changes things. Jim Gatlin should be here. Where the hell is he?'

'When those four fellers quit haggling over another man's fortune and move out of here, he's in trouble,' Kitty said. 'With Green and Mundt in town for their Saturday night on the prairie dew, your cousin persuaded Josh now was as good a time as any to go talk to a man about a train robbery.'

Pine swore softly. 'If this had come up before they left . . . '

'But it didn't,' Kitty said. 'So now we put that right.'

'We?'

'That's right. Wait there and keep your eye on those four.'

She slid down off the stool, tossed

the cloth under the bar and, with a nod to the barman, headed for the stairs.

Time dragged on. After five minutes, Pine was getting itchy. The four men at the table finished their discussion. With River and Hidalgo leading the way they banged out of the saloon with a deadly purpose in their stride.

Pine waited until the sound of horses announced the men's departure, then followed them in haste but only as far as the door. From there he watched them ride down the hill and swing out of sight at the corner by the bank.

They were, he guessed, about to converge on the jail. He wondered if Josh Notion had followed the dead marshal's habit of leaving old Ned Riley minding the store.

Pine spent the next five minutes calming jumpy nerves by trying to imagine what the blonde saloonist would look like in the garb of a night rider. It was time wasted. Kitty Mac still hadn't appeared when Pine heard the sound of a distant shot. A heavy blast, probably from a shotgun. He was away from the bar in an instant and looking impatiently at the stairs when the crack of a second shot split the night air.

★ ★ ★

'Go get Wilson,' River said.

'Sure,' Hidalgo said, grinning. He grabbed the ring from the hook and went through to the cell block, boots slapping, keys jingling.

Mundt was flat on the floor of the marshal's office, one leg twitching, his face a pulpy mass of bone and blood. Behind Jax Silva's desk old Ned Riley was slumped in the chair, rheumy eyes narrowed as he held a hand to a bloody upper arm. The shotgun he had used to kill Mundt was on the desk, a curl of smoke still issuing from the muzzles.

Green was holding a six-gun on the old deputy. His eyes were furious. One slim, gloved hand was opening and closing restlessly at his side.

'No more,' River told him. 'It's all over when we've got Wilson out.' His smile was twisted. 'Besides, losing your partner means your share just went up.'

Then Wilson came ducking through the doorway from the the cell block ahead of Hidalgo. His fair hair was all over the place from lying on the cot. He looked around for his gunbelt, found it, buckled it on. He stepped over Mundt, lying still now with his head in a pool of blood, looked at the fuming Green.

'What's he doing here?'

Behind him Hidalgo said, 'He's our new partner, the one who will show us the way to the money. We had two, but the other man carelessly stepped in front of the old deputy's shotgun.'

'You mean he's taking us to the Hood spread?' Wilson swung on Green. 'You can do that?'

'For a price.'

'Sure. Why would a man help someone for nothing?'

His head swung around as the sound of hoofs drifted to them from across the street. Hidalgo had already sprung to the open door.

'The Pinkerton man with the blonde woman from the saloon,' he said. 'Heading out of town *muy rápido*.' His teeth flashed. 'I think she has on her father's clothes.'

'You've all just come down from the saloon,' Wilson said. 'You were up there talking, so what I think is maybe you talked too damn loud.'

River glowered. 'Never mind how loud we talked. We've broke the deadlock while you've been enjoying a goddamn vacation, come *a long way* without you . . . '

'Without me you'd still be in southern Texas drinking bad mescal and scratchin' for your next dollar,' Wilson said with contempt. He looked at Hidalgo. 'Which way were those two going?'

The 'breed jerked a thumb to the south-west. 'Heading into the foothills up against the Big Horns.'

Wilson looked at Green. 'That the

way to the Hood place?'

'It's the way to a lot of places.'

'But only one where the old train robber you're about to double-cross stashed his fortune.' He found his hat, slapped it on his head and said, 'Come on, let's all go and get rich.'

18

Thin clouds had slipped away from a crescent moon when Gatlin turned his horse off the trail to follow Josh Notion onto a long drive leading up to a house where lamplight glowed in downstairs windows shaded by wide verandas.

'Tall Timbers,' Notion said. 'Fancy name for a fancy spread bought and flourishing on stolen money — correct?'

'It's correct, and that's what Hood will be forced to admit when I confront him.'

'Then what?'

'You already know what. Then nothing — because that as far as my thinking's gone.'

'Thinking, or dreaming?'

Gatlin smiled in the wan light. 'It was a dream for eight years, Josh. Then, helped by Charlie Pine, I found Hood

206

— and suddenly I woke up and the dream was real.'

'All right.' Notion rode on up the slope towards the house in silence. Then he said, 'I think now's the time to hand over your pistol.'

'What if I say there'll be no violence? My word not good enough?'

'Your word's good, but I'm not so sure about your self-control. The times I've spoken to Hood — a long time ago, mind you — he could be an abrasive character inclined to treat other folk and their feelings with disdain. He'll get your hackles up, no question — and knowing the torment you've been through that's when I'll feel a lot happier with your pistol tucked in my belt.'

They had almost reached the house, the lights spilling from the windows warm on the gravel, the verandas looming dark overhead. Without a word Gatlin drew his six-gun and handed it to Notion butt first. Even as he was doing so, the front door opened and a tall man stepped out. He was outlined by the lamplight. Gatlin saw that he was using a cane for support. The man had obviously caught the movement, seen the light glinting on the pistol's barrel as the weapon changed hands . . .

Gatlin drew his horse to a halt, heard Notion do the same a little way behind him. So he can watch me, Gatlin thought. Step in fast if I go beserk. He looked hard at the tall man. He was standing in watchful silence. Gatlin didn't recognize him.

'I'm here to see Nathan Hood,' he said. 'You are . . . ?'

'Nate's brother, Tom Hood.'

'Tell your brother Jim Gatlin wants to talk to him — '

Gatlin broke off as a woman brushed past Tom Hood. Young, dark hair — he knew this must be Belinda Hood. His pulse quickened. After ten years he was another step closer.

'You're Jim Gatlin. And you want to see my father?'

'That's right, ma'am.'

She visibly took a deep breath. 'Yes, all right. I'll take you to him — '

'Belinda — '

'No, it's all right.' She touched her uncle's arm. 'It really is all right, Tom, I'll take Mr Gatlin to see my father and then it'll be over and . . . '

She broke off. Her eyes were too bright. Gatlin thought he caught the glint of a tear. Then she turned away and as she walked gracefully across the front of the house he swung down and hurried to catch up with her.

'Where is he?'

'Out back.'

'I'm unarmed. And I give you my word I won't harm him.' He hesitated, fumbling for the right words. 'I came not knowing what I wanted, but now I'm here I think all I've ever wanted is an admission — '

She stopped walking and swung on him. 'Of what?'

'Guilt. I want to hear that from your father. I want that — and an apology — '

'You will never get either from Nathan Hood,' she said bluntly, and once again she was walking quickly away from him.

She led him around the house into the shadows of a back garden surrounded by tall trees and Gatlin thought absently that here, from this garden and these trees, this was where the house got its name and then he frowned. Belinda Hood was crossing the garden, away from the house and dimly seen outbuildings. Ahead of her there was a gate in a white picket fence, beyond it angular shapes picked out by the pale light of the moon. Shapes Gatlin recognized with feelings of utter disbelief.

And then the young woman had opened the gate and stepped through and when Gatlin followed, reluctantly now, she was standing in front of a plain, white wooden cross.

He knew they were in the family cemetery. Without thinking, he removed his hat.

'My father killed himself a year ago,' Belinda said, speaking so quietly that Gatlin had to strain to hear. 'He killed himself when he knew you'd been released from prison. I think he knew what you would do, was terrified — '

'Then he was wrong,' Gatlin said huskily.

'He'd been wrong before, hadn't he?' Belinda said, and there was a tired smile on her pale face. 'He knew he'd been wrong — '

'Yes,' Gatlin cut in, and suddenly he felt a flood of relief, an incredible feeling of release. 'Yes, he did,' he said, and in his relief the words came tumbling out. 'He did know, and when you said a few minutes ago that I would never get an admission of guilt from your father — you were wrong, too, because that's what this was, that's what this is, he took his own life not because he was frightened but because — '

They were both interrupted by a sudden shout. When Gatlin looked back he saw a man coming around the side of the house.

It was Charlie Pine.

*   ★   ★

'There was shooting down at the jail,' Pine said. 'I reckon they got Wilson out. We're ahead of them but only just.'

They had rushed around the house then, Gatlin, Pine and Belinda. Tom Hood had limped back inside. The door was shut. Kitty Mac was talking to Josh Notion. Gatlin found himself looking at a very different Kitty Mac. Appearing slimmer, she was wearing trousers tucked into stovepipe boots and a plaid mackinaw to keep out the night chill. She was carrying a rifle in soft hands that usually served drinks.

'Ahead of who?' Gatlin said. 'If you're talking about those Texans, they don't know where Hood — '

'They'll know now. Green and Mundt are siding with Wilson, River and Hidalgo.'

'I never trusted them,' Belinda said. 'I've always wondered why they stayed after my father . . . died.'

There was astonishment in the looks Kitty Mac and Notion threw in her direction. Then, the shock revelation of Hood's death accepted, it was time for fast thinking.

'They'll know the way here from Green and Mundt,' Notion said, 'but they'll also know there's nobody here can stand in their way.'

'I rode past the jail with Kitty,' Pine said ruefully. 'Hidalgo was watching.'

'OK, so they'll be thinking you, Kitty, Tom Hood and Belinda.'

Pine nodded. 'Enough to give them pause.'

'No. Tom's lame,' Belinda said. 'I . . . can't shoot well. They know that . . . '

She turned to look down the long drive as the drum of approaching hoofs was carried to them on the light breeze.

'Four,' Gatlin said, peering through narrowed eyes as distant riders hove into view. 'There should be five.'

'Getting Wilson out of jail,' Notion said, 'must have cost them a man. But where the hell does that leave old Ned?'

'He'll save for later,' Gatlin said, and managed a grin. 'You'd have to wake him up to kill him.' Then he sobered. 'Belinda, Kitty, you go into the house — '

'Not me,' Kitty said, and brandished the rifle. 'You want me to shoot them out of the saddle, I'll do that now.'

Gatlin looked around, saw trees over to his left and cast a fast glance down the drive to the four approaching riders. 'All right, Kitty, stay. You take the far side of the house with Josh. Charlie, we'll use those trees for cover.'

'Sure,' Notion said, already moving away with the blonde saloonist. 'But when they get here, hold your fire. It's up to me as the law to sing out a challenge and act on their response . . .'

The door slammed as Belinda Hood hurried into the house. Gatlin watched Notion and Kitty Mac sprint for the trees. Then he followed Charlie Pine to the stand of trees on the eastern side of the grounds. He knew they must have been seen by the outlaws. That didn't make the cover any less effective. The approaching riders would know that drawing nearer would put them in a possible crossfire. Give them pause was right . . .

'They're slowing,' Pine said as Gatlin joined him inside the trees and drew his six-gun.

'Can you see who's missing?'

'Mundt.'

'Wait for Josh. He'll holler. That's if they get close — '

Then a rifle cracked.

One of the oncoming riders went backwards out of the saddle. The riderless horse swerved, then trotted away across the rich grass.

'Christ!' Pine said, 'that was Wilson.'

'And the only person I saw carrying a rifle was Kitty Mac.'

'Take the leader,' Pine said, 'and the others will back off. I think our Kitty figured that out for herself and disobeyed orders.'

Pine, Gatlin saw, had got it only part right. Green was already out of it: he wheeled his horse and raced back down the moonlit drive. But River wasn't finished. He swung an arm and yelled orders. Then he crouched low in the saddle and spurred his horse towards the trees sheltering Notion and Kitty Mac. Hidalgo spun his horse towards Gatlin and Pine. He came at them like an Indian. His left leg was hooked over the saddle horn. He hung down, clinging to his mount's right flank, and blasted shots from under its straining neck.

Gunfire rattled from across the grounds where River was attacking Notion's position. As Hidalgo bore down on them Gatlin heard hot lead snicking through the overhead branches. Then there was a meaty thud. Charlie Pine gasped. Brush crackled as he fell across Gatlin's feet. Gatlin glanced down, saw dark blood on Pine's shirt. He crouched, gently eased the Pinkerton man's dead weight into a comfortable position on the dead leaves.

'Hang on, Charlie,' he said — then jerked his head up to locate the outlaw.

Hidalgo was on him. Teeth gleaming, the 'breed unhooked his leg from the horn. He hit the ground rolling as the horse veered away. Gatlin leaped out of the trees. Slugs hissed past his head as Hidalgo came to his knees and snapped wild shots. Then Gatlin's first, carefully aimed shot took the 'breed in the chest. His eyes widened. Breath gurgled in his throat. The gleaming white teeth darkened with blood. The outlaw sank to the ground, groaning.

On the other side of the house, a third body lay crumpled on the grass and another riderless horse trotted away as gunsmoke drifted. The three horses came together in the moonlight, stood nervously with trailing reins as Notion and Kitty Mac came out of the trees.

Josh Notion's authority had been

217

usurped by the woman who for many years had stood by him to resist one powerful man's takeover of a sleep town. His challenge had never been uttered, the fight taken out of his hands and settled by a woman with a rifle and an ex-convict who had come to confront Nathan Hood and ended up defending his daughter.

Josh Notion had his arm around Kitty Mac's shoulder. No hard feelings. As Gatlin watched, the gunsmith bent and planted a kiss on her cheek.

It was over.

But in the cold moonlight, all Jim Gatlin felt was — empty.

19

It was Belinda Hood who suggested using the top buggy to take the dead and the wounded into Cedar Creek. She drove it herself, with Charlie Pine sitting hunched but cheerful by her side and Gatlin, Kitty Mac and Notion outriders offering words of encouragement.

They pulled in outside the jail. Notion rushed inside to check on Ned Riley and found the deputy drinking coffee with his own bandanna tied around a bloody wound and a grin on his lined old face as he watched over the outlaw he had killed.

The undertaker was summoned, and took away the bodies. The doctor came down to the jail and tended to Charlie Pine's shoulder wound. Kitty Mac reverted to the role of saloonist, located Jax Silva's bottle of whiskey and poured raw spirit into as many tin cups as she could find while the town's one-eyed, temporary marshal tried to look officious. Without much success.

Gatlin drank with little enthusiasm. The emptiness had stayed with him. Ten years ago he had heard rumours that sent him on the run, had been tried and convicted of a crime he had not committed and served eight years of a ten-year sentence. During all that time he had been sustained by intoxicating dreams of retribution. Twelve months after his release he had located the man whose crime he had served time for — only to discover that the man had been dead by his own hand for a full year.

He would never know why he had been framed.

'It was Tom's idea to keep the death secret,' Belinda said, in answer to his question. 'Alone, a rich man's daughter would be vulnerable. Nathan's power kept people away when he was alive. As long as people *believed* he was alive, that power remained.'

Gatlin nodded. He could feel Charlie Pine's eyes on him.

'If life seems empty,' Pine said, unerringly reading Gatlin's mind, 'do something to fill it.'

'Like what?'

'What you did when you went after Nathan Hood was good investigative work.'

'With your help.'

'It's called teamwork. I can get in touch with my boss, Charlie Eames. Ride with me to Denver. The Pinkertons could use a man with your . . . rare talents.'

That one finally brought a grin to Gatlin's face. 'What are you saying Charlie? That I understand the criminal mind?'

'Well,' the Pinkerton man said, 'if you don't understand the way those fellers tick after eight years in the pen — then I'll be damned if I know who does.'

We do hope that you have enjoyed reading this large print book.

Did you know that all of our titles are available for purchase?

We publish a wide range of high quality large print books including:
Romances, Mysteries, Classics
General Fiction
Non Fiction and Westerns

Special interest titles available in large print are:
The Little Oxford Dictionary
Music Book, Song Book
Hymn Book, Service Book

Also available from us courtesy of Oxford University Press:
Young Readers' Dictionary
(large print edition)
Young Readers' Thesaurus
(large print edition)

For further information or a free brochure, please contact us at:
Ulverscroft Large Print Books Ltd.,
The Green, Bradgate Road, Anstey,
Leicester, LE7 7FU, England.
Tel: (00 44) **0116 236 4325**
Fax: (00 44) **0116 234 0205**

BUCK AND THE WIDOW RANCHER

Carlton Youngblood

When James Buckley Armstrong comes to help a recently widowed woman, somebody welcomes him with a deadly ambush. The young widow faces many problems: her husband was killed, then gambling IOUs showed up. Now a bank loan is due, and rustlers are stealing her herd. Not knowing where to start, Buck is ambushed again and beaten unconscious — and then he gets mad. Waking up with no water, no hat and no horse makes Buck ready to even the score.

TALMAN'S WAR

Richard Wyler

Jim Talman figured he had trouble enough with drought drying up his water and threatening his herds. That was until Philip Olsen, a man greedy for land, cast his eyes on the Talman range. Jim soon found that talk wouldn't solve the problem — and realised that the only way to hold onto his land was to fight for it.